Delvecchio's Brooklyn

DELVECCHIO'S BROOKLYN

A Short Story Collection

With an introduction by Max Allan Collins

Robert J. Randisi

Five Star
Unity, Maine

Additional copyright information on page 207.

Five Star First Edition Mystery Series.

First Edition, Second Printing

Published in 2001 in conjunction with
Tekno Books and Ed Gorman.

Cover design by Carol Pringle.

Set in 11 pt. Plantin by Rick Gundberg.

Printed in the United States on permanent paper.

Library of Congress Cataloging-in-Publication Data

Randisi, Robert J.
　Delvecchio's Brooklyn : a short story collection / by
Robert J. Randisi ; with an introduction by Max Allan
Collins.
　　p.　cm.
　　Contents: The snaphaunce — A matter of ethics — The
vanishing virgin — Double edge — Turnabout — Laying
down to die — A favor for Sam — Like a stranger — The
old dons.
　　ISBN 0-7862-3044-4 (hc : alk. paper)
　　1. Delvecchio, Nick (Fictitious character) — Fiction.
2. Private investigators — New York (State) — New York —
Fiction.　3. Detective and mystery stories, American.
4. Brooklyn (New York, N.Y.) — Fiction.　I. Title.
PS3568.A53 D45 2001
　813'.54—dc21
　　　　　　　　　　　　　　　　　　　　　　00-051066

Table of Contents

Fast and Good

An Introduction by Max Allan Collins

My friend Bob Randisi is widely known in the mystery trade as the fastest writer in the business—in fact, he takes a lot of good-natured ribbing about his speed and facility from his peers, all of whom are amazed and no doubt envious.

But it's no accomplishment to just be fast—what makes Randisi special is that he is also good. A typical description of a Randisi novel or story—"a good, fast read"—is also a description of how Bob writes.

Under a pseudonym, Bob has written hundreds—that's no typo—of western novels, mostly in a series that is one of the longest running and most successful of its kind. Bob is in a long tradition of good, fast writers—Erle Stanley Gardner and John Creasy come to mind (Mickey Spillane, too, though the Mick is not prolific, just fast)—who capitalize on a natural storytelling gift and an enthusiasm for the writing craft to fashion dialogue-driven, action-packed narratives. Like that trio of authors, Randisi does not stint on character and knows that character is tied to action (and that dialogue is a form of action).

Though Bob's greatest commercial success has been in the western field, his first and truest love is the mystery novel, specifically, the private eye story. All three of his detectives (Po, Jacoby—who do not appear in this collection—and Delvecchio) have appeared in Randisi novels (Bob frequently "tries out" an idea for a novel in the compact short story form) and typically reflect personal interests of his—often sports, such as racing (Po) and boxing (Jacoby)—and each detective is at once a version of Randisi himself and yet a distinct unto-himself protagonist. (Bob's background in police work is reflected in his many glowingly reviewed non-P.I. novels.)

The irony of Bob's career is that he has become an extremely successful writer outside the mystery field, while his best-known contribution to his beloved private eye genre is his founding of the writers' organization, the Private Eye Writers of America (the source of the famous and respected "Shamus" awards). The prominence of this writers' organization has, unfortunately, overshadowed recognition due Bob as one of the finest writers of private eye fiction of the late twentieth (and now early twenty-first) century.

A while back both Bob and I were invited to contribute to an anthology celebrating the 100th birthday of Raymond Chandler—the writers were to pen new Philip Marlowe short stories. We both felt honored to be included among many of the top names in the field, and that book generated a lot of good comments from reviewers and readers alike, and was recently reprinted in trade paperback—it's fair to say that it's one of the most important anthologies of recent years.

And there were a lot of good stories in that book, as no mystery writer wants to look bad in an anthology celebrating a master of the form (and his most famous creation). I felt some of the writers—some of the best ones—tried too hard, at times lapsing into painful pastiche. But I was nevertheless proud to be in such company, and took my best shot, writing what I still feel is one of my best stories.

But the best story in the book was by a guy named Randisi. And I think it was the best, in part, because Bob is a working writer, in the blue-collar pulp tradition, and was not intimidated by the notion of writing a Chandler/Marlowe story—hell, he had the private eye novel in his blood (having taken transfusions since childhood) and so he just stepped up to the plate and knocked the ball out of the park. (That tale is not included here, as it does not feature a Randisi-created detective; but it's worth looking for—as you'll realize after you read this collection.) Bob was the first fellow writer with whom I became friendly—he was also the first human being outside my immediate family I ever met who had read my first two books! So I will be forgiven a certain bias in his favor.

He is a hell of a guy—but also a hell of a writer.

I'm confident that when you read these P.I. tales, you will fast discover just how good this guy Randisi is.

The Snaphaunce

When I read about the double murder in the newspapers, it made me think back a week . . .

My name is Nick Delvecchio and I'm a private investigator, or what people generally refer to as a private eye. I operate a one-man agency out of Brooklyn, on Sackett Street, walking distance from the Brooklyn Bridge. I've often been told that I was a fool not to open my office across the bridge in Manhattan. But I was born and raised in Brooklyn and I felt I should stay on my own turf. I know Flatbush Avenue better than I know Fifth Avenue, and I know Atlantic Avenue and Court Street better than I know Madison Avenue and Wall Street.

I'm a Brooklyn boy and will probably always be one—although thirty-four is far from being a boy.

After the incident that got me pensioned off the police department, I had to find something that would allow me to keep doing the things I enjoyed doing. The same "hook" or "rabbi" that got me off the job with a one-third pension instead of a prison sentence also got me my investigator's license. That was five years ago.

People generally call me when something is missing. That has turned out to be the bulk of my business. You'd be surprised at some of the things I've been hired to find: cats, dogs, matching bookends, people—twins, once—and one time a truckload of dirt. See, there was something buried . . . but that's another story.

Sorry, nary a falcon in the lot. But then I never claimed to be Sam Spade. I'm just trying to make a living the best way I know how.

This time around, it was a gun.

The message came to me via my second-hand telephone answering machine, which I had picked up in lieu of a fee from a client who had more problems than cash.

It was from a Mr. Higgins—the message, that is, not the machine—who asked if I could come out to his home on Long Island to discuss the possible engagement of my services. Honest, that's just what he said. He sounded like money, though, so I figured, why not take a ride?

The Higgins home turned out to be an estate, which was something of a shock—culture shock—to a street kid like me. The door was opened by a faded lady of class. She appeared to be in her mid-forties and, although quite well preserved and handsome, her best days were definitely behind her—and she knew it.

"I'd like to see Mr. Higgins, please?" I asked politely. I'm always polite to people I like, or people I've never met before.

"Oh," she replied, as if I had identified myself as the garbage man and said I was making a delivery. "You must be the private detective Stuart called."

"Yes, ma'am," I admitted. "My name is Delvecchio."

I showed her my I.D. and she was unimpressed, possibly even displeased. She couldn't disguise the resigned slump of her shoulders or the faint sigh that escaped her dry lips.

"Come in then," she said finally, backing up to allow me room to do so. She closed the door and added, "He's in the gun room. I'll take you to him."

"Thank you."

As she led the way down a long, deep-pile carpeted hallway, I said, "The gun room?"

12

"My husband loves guns, Mr. Delvecchio," she explained wearily. "He spends all his time and passion on guns, and has done so for years."

It sounded like an old complaint. I didn't try to carry the conversation further because I thought she might be in the market for a shoulder to cry on, and I wasn't willing to offer mine.

She stopped before a large oak door and opened it without knocking. She did it as if it were an act of defiance.

"Stuart," I heard her say with her back to me, "your detective is here."

She stepped aside then to let me go past her. The man in the room was tall, thin, and silver-haired. Somewhere between fifty and sixty—either a good sixty, or a piss poor fifty. He was surrounded by guns of every conceivable size and shape, some contained in glass cases, many of them adorning the walls, hanging on hooks . . .

"Mr. Delvecchio?" he asked.

"That's right."

He approached me with his hand outstretched. I took it and he said, "I am Stuart Higgins. Thank you for coming." His eyes flicked momentarily to his wife and he told her, "That will be all, Libby."

Arbitrarily dismissed, she left the room. I was almost embarrassed for her, but she was obviously used to it. She left without a word, closing the door softly behind her. Her defiance apparently did not carry to the point of door slamming.

"I'm happy you were able to come," Higgins said when she had gone. "I hate talking to those damnable telephone machines—I usually hang up when they answer—but this time I'm glad I did. Can I get you a drink?"

"No, thank you. I'd like to get to why you asked me out here." I couldn't help being short with him. I said before that

I'm polite to people I've just met, but there are exceptions to every rule.

"To the point," he said, walking to the sideboard and picking up a drink he had obviously already started. "I like that." He faced me head on then and said, "I am missing a snaphaunce."

"A what?"

"I'm sorry," he said, looking confused. "You're a private eye, I thought you would know about guns."

"That's a gun?" I asked. "A snap . . . what?"

"Snap*haunce*." He put his drink down and walked over to one of his display cases. "I'll show you," he said, reaching in and removing a gun. He turned and held it out to me. "This is a snaphaunce."

What I saw was a gun I would expect to see old Dan'l Boone carrying on TV, with Ed Ames at his side.

"It's late sixteenth century," Higgins explained, which put me in my place. "No one quite knows for sure but the general feeling is that it had its origin in Germany." I could see that he was warming to his subject. His eyes were glowing and there was a light sheen of perspiration on his forehead and upper lip.

"It is a derivative of the German 'Schnapphahn', or 'snapping hammer'," he continued. "As it became more popular throughout Europe, local peculiarities began to pop up. The one you are holding is the Swedish or Baltic version, which is characterized by this extremely long arm and jaw to the cock, you see, which appears—"

"Excuse me," I said, to forestall getting further into the lecture, "but now that I have an idea of what it is, do you suppose we could get back to the one that you're missing?"

"I'm sorry," he said, taking the gun back from my dirty, unappreciative hands, "I thought that perhaps its history might be of some help." He put it back in the display case and then turned to face me again.

"The one I am missing," he began stiffly, "is the brother of that one." He pointed to one on the wall and I could see that there was an empty hook right next to it. He removed the one that was still there and, making no move to hand it to me this time, simply held it out to show me. It appeared to be somewhat smaller than the one he had previously been showing me.

"The two are identical, late eighteenth century. As you can see from this one, they are pocket pistols. Both are inlaid with mounts of chiseled iron and silver."

"Are they valuable?"

"Ordinarily, yes, and even more so to the collector. This in particular is very valuable to me because it is part of a set." He fondled the one in his hand and said, "I want my snaphaunce back, Mr. Delvecchio."

I looked around the room. There were no windows and no other doors. All four walls were covered with guns, and there were several display cases of them, from the sixteenth century model he had shown me, to the more modern.

I knew it would have taken a fortune to amass a collection like that.

"All right, Mr. Higgins, I'll look for your snaphaunce for you. Can you give me some idea of who might have wanted to steal it?"

"I would have thought it was a burglar," he said, frowning.

"A burglar would not have gained entry to your house and simply taken one gun."

"Snaphaunce."

"Whatever. Was there anything else taken? Silverware, your wife's jewelry, for instance?"

"No, nothing."

"Then whoever gained entry obviously knew what they wanted."

"If they knew what they wanted," Higgins said, "they would have broken into one of the display cases and taken a more valuable item."

"Then we're dealing with someone who wanted a gun, and wasn't particular about which one they took."

What I couldn't figure out was why they hadn't taken a more modern, usable gun if they needed one so badly. Obviously, the need for "a" gun was not for one that could be used.

"Can you think of anyone?"

He frowned again and then said, "I'm sorry . . ."

"Who knew you had these two particular pistols in your collection?"

"Well, the entire gun club, I imagine. I didn't keep their purchase a secret."

"Were they purchased recently?"

He made a face and said, "Last week. I've only had them a week." He said it as if he were discussing two infants, one of which had suffered a crib death.

"Who else lives in this house?"

"Just Libby, my wife."

"No servants," I asked, "in a house this large?"

"None that live here."

"I see. And no children?"

"We never had any," he said in a "who needs them?" tone of voice.

"Where is the gun club you belong to?"

"I belong to several. An antique gun club here on Long Island, and a gun club in the city." He named them and gave me the addresses. The one in Manhattan was in mid-town, on 43rd Street and Second Avenue. I knew the place, but had never been inside. Guns for fun aren't my style, although I owned several from my cop days.

"Do you carry a gun, Mr. Delvecchio?" Higgins asked.

I was glad he'd asked me that instead of if I owned one, because then I would have had to answer yes.

"No, Mr. Higgins, I don't carry a gun," I said, and watched with relish as his face fell.

He frowned, probably wondering if he had hired the right guy.

"They're beautiful things, you know," he said, fondling the one he was holding, "made all the more so by the fact they are deadly."

"I'm sure."

We discussed my fee and he gave me a check for $150— one day—as a retainer. I tucked it away in my shirt pocket and told him I'd be in touch as soon as I had something to report.

"I'll have Libby show you out," he offered, walking to his desk and pressing an intercom button. She opened the door to the room a few seconds later.

"Show Mr. Delvecchio out, my dear."

"This way," she said to me.

On the way to the front door she said, "I suppose you're going to try and find the damned gun for him."

"Yes, ma'am."

"He wouldn't have hired you if it was I who was missing," she observed at the door and then shut it leaving me on the front steps to ponder the remark.

I pondered something else as well. I wondered about the fact that Mrs. Higgins had changed her clothes since I had arrived, and added a fresh dose of make-up and perfume.

The lady was going out . . . and soon.

I'm a great believer in hunches, so I played one.

I waited in my car by the front gates of the Higgins estate, and I didn't have long to wait. In a matter of minutes the gates swung open and a red Ferrari drove out. I started my six-year-old Oldsmobile and hoped I'd be able to keep up. It turned out not to be a problem. The car had a lot of potential, but she used practically none of it.

To make a long trip short, she led me to 43rd and Second Avenue, right to her husband's gun club. After she left the car in a parking lot she came out wearing dark glasses and kerchief and went into the building that housed the club. I parked illegally and followed her, hoping I'd be back out before they towed the car.

On entering the building, I discovered that the place was also a health club.

"Yes?" the young lady at the front desk asked. "May I help you?"

"You sure can. Uh, my wife wants me to buy a gun, but I don't think it's a very good idea."

She smiled patiently—and prettily—and said, "Guns can be very helpful."

"Oh, I know that. What I mean is, it's not a good idea until I learn how to use one."

"You're absolutely right—" she began, but she was interrupted as a door behind her opened and voices became audible.

". . . shouldn't have come straight here," a man was saying.

"I'm sorry, darling—" Libby Higgins was responding as she came out, but she stopped short when she saw me, her mouth open.

The man behind her was in his mid-forties, good looking despite a receding hairline and a somewhat weak chin. He was dressed to show off his physique: T-shirt with short

18

sleeves, making his bulging biceps plainly visible and tight enough to show the ridge of his pectorals. Unfortunately he was also starting to thicken around the middle, and the shirt showed this as well.

"Sir?" the girl behind the desk was calling me. "Excuse me, sir . . ."

"I'll take care of the gentleman, Sue," the guy in the T-shirt said, quick to assess the situation. "Would you come into my office please?" he asked me.

He ushered Libby Higgins back into his office and I followed them inside.

"My name is Charles Logan, Mr. . . . Delvecchio, is it?"

"That's right."

He put on a worldly smile and said, "I suppose there's no denying what you heard and saw."

I shrugged and said, "I didn't *see* anything."

"But you heard enough."

"I heard enough to tell me that you and Mrs. Higgins aren't just friends."

"We're lovers, Mr. Delvecchio, and we're not ashamed of it," he said, inflating his manly chest to even greater proportions. "Stuart thinks of nothing but his gun collection, and Libby is a healthy, lovely, vibrant woman. What happened was not something we planned," he explained, "but it did."

"Well, that's fine, Mr. Logan," I said. "I'm all for love, believe me, but Mr. Higgins has hired me to retrieve his property." Ignoring him and directing myself to my client's wife: "Mrs. Higgins, why did you take his snaphaunce?"

"Take his—" she began, not understanding.

"The gun, dear," Logan told her. "I know of a buyer who will pay a great deal for the snaphaunce, Mr. Delvecchio, and we need the money to get away together."

"Who is the buyer?"

19

"I don't think that's imp—" Logan began, but I cut him off before he could go any further.

"It's Higgins, isn't it?" I asked. "I mean, who would pay more than he would. What good is one without the other, right?"

Logan frowned, annoyed that I had seen through his lie.

"You're a smartass, Delvecchio, right?" he asked, sounding less like a gentleman all of a sudden and more like a kid from Brooklyn. "All right, so we were going to sell it back to him and then take off. Now I suppose you'll tell him who has it, and he'll file charges against me."

"I don't think so," I said. "You didn't steal it, his wife did. I think if you turn it over to me, he'll forget the whole incident. All he wants is his property back."

"Mr. Delvecchio," Libby Higgins spoke up, "do you have to tell him where you found it? Must you tell him about . . . us?"

I didn't really have to, and probably wouldn't have if Logan hadn't decided to get aggressive and nasty about it.

"Sure he will," he sneered. "He gets his kicks that way, don't you, private eye? Just like looking through keyholes, isn't it?"

"Back off, Logan."

"Oh, really?" he said. "Back off? What if I decide to break you in half, Delvecchio?" he asked, taking a step toward me.

While on the police force, and in uniform, I had been attacked by three men and given a terrible beating. After I had recovered and gotten back into uniform, I swore I'd never take a beating again. From anybody. Before anyone could do me serious injury, I'd be the one dishing it out. That attitude had gotten me kicked off the force after an incident that had resulted in an injury to a prominent politician's son who thought it would be smart to hit a cop.

The result of that—thanks to a friend with some influence—had been the one-third pension and the P.I's license, in order to avoid scandal.

Charles Logan, however, did not look like a prominent man's son, and although he was about ten years older than I was, he outweighed me considerably. Still, I had no intentions of taking a beating from him either.

"Logan, I won't fight with you—"

"I know that," he said, smugly.

"—I'll just shoot off one of your kneecaps if you take another step," I finished.

He had been about to take one and stopped short. He apparently couldn't tell whether or not I was wearing a gun, but the private eye mystique worked in my favor for once. He *assumed* I had one, and further, that I would use it.

He backed off.

He was right, in a sense. If I had been carrying a gun, I would have used it rather than take a beating.

"Would you give me the snaphaunce, please?" I asked, putting my left hand out.

Logan glared at me, probably wishing he had the nerve to call my bluff, then looked at Libby Higgins, who nodded with tears in her eyes. He stepped back behind his desk, opened one of the drawers and took out the snaphaunce. It was identical to the one Higgins had shown me.

"Thank you," I said, taking it from him. A pocket pistol, Higgins had called it, but it seemed a bit bulky for that to me. I slipped it under my waistband instead.

As I started for the door, Mrs. Higgins called out to me.

"Mr. Delvecchio."

"Yes, Mrs. Higgins?"

"Do you have to tell Stuart . . ."

"He's my client," I answered.

21

Logan put his hand on her arm, as if to tell her not to worry, their love would see them through.

I hoped it would—for her sake, not his—but I didn't owe either of them a thing. My allegiance had to be to the man who was paying me—even if I didn't like him.

. . . so when I read the story in the papers, I went back over the entire affair again.

The story in the papers was about a man and a woman who were found shot to death in the man's apartment. Apparently the woman was married, and she and the man were having an affair. Naturally her husband was questioned, but he wasn't held. He was a rich, prominent man, with his fingers in a lot of pies.

Coincidence is a funny thing. It was while I had the newspaper on my desk, reading the story, that I found the envelope from Higgins in my morning mail. I split it open, finished reading the story, then took out the check for five thousand dollars. It was made out to me with "for services" written on the bottom left hand corner, on the memo line.

What services? I had already been paid for returning his damn gun, the very same day I had brought it back to him and told him the story of how it came to be missing. He'd nodded to himself, taken the gun from me, fondled it, wrote me a check for my fee, thanked me and bade me good day. I showed myself out.

Now, on the same day that I read about a double murder, I received a second check for substantially more than my normal fee.

For services.

For keeping my mouth shut, was more like it.

I picked up the phone, dialed the number for the Seven-

teenth Precinct in Manhattan and asked for Detective
Wright.

"This is Nick Delvecchio, Detective Wright," I said. "Remember me?"

"Uh, sure, the private eye from across the bridge. How're
things in Brooklyn?"

"Fine."

"What can I do for you?"

"The double murder that hit the papers today."

"The love nest thing?" he asked. "What have you got to do
with that?"

"I did a job for the husband last week. I think he's good for
it, Wright."

"We questioned him, Delvecchio. You know, him being
the husband and all, he was the first suspect. He had a
story—"

"A good one?"

"He said he kicked his old lady out a few days ago. Knew
all about the affair, but he didn't seem all that upset about it. I
don't think he gave a damn about her so why would he kill
them? Pride? Guys with that much money don't need pride.
You saying he loved her?"

Pride? I didn't think so, either. Love? No way. I knew the
real reason he'd killed them. Mrs. Higgins had told me that
day at the house. "My husband loves guns."

"No, Wright, he didn't love her," I said, folding the check
neatly in half.

"Then why did he kill them?"

I tore the check in two and allowed the equal parts to
flutter to the desk before answering.

"They took his snaphaunce."

A Matter of Ethics

I got mugged on the way to meet a potential client.

Well, actually it wasn't really a "mugging," but more of an "asking."

My car was in the shop and I wasn't able to borrow one, so there I was taking the subway to meet with Mrs. Alex Randolph, who lived in the Canarsie section of Brooklyn. I hadn't been on the subway in years, having studiously avoided it.

I had switched to the double-L train—which I would ride to the last stop in Canarsie—when I was approached by a tall, young black lad who asked me for my wallet. When I refused he said he'd cut me. He asked me for my wallet again and I asked to see his knife. He showed it to me, and I gave him my wallet. It was a simple transaction. He got my wallet and I got to keep—well, whatever it was he would have cut off. The thirteen dollars in my wallet and one credit card that hadn't been taken away from me yet were not enough to get cut, or possibly killed, for.

So when I reached the last stop I was penniless, and the "asker" had gotten off the train ten or twelve stops back. There was no point in looking for a cop, so I simply walked to the address Mrs. Randolph had given me on 95th Street and rang the bell, determined to take the job whatever it was and get a retainer so I could take a cab back to my apartment/office on Sackett Street.

The woman who answered the door was handsomely ap-

25

proaching forty. She looked me up and down and asked, "Mr. Delvecchio?"

"That's right."

"Come in, please."

The house was huge and old and I had the feeling that she had lived there a long time. We went through a foyer into a living room, where she offered me a seat and nothing more. I could have used a drink after my experience on the train, but didn't mention it.

"Mr. Delvecchio, the job I want to hire you for is a very simple one, but it might sound strange to you."

"I've had a lot of strange jobs in my time, Mrs. Randolph."

"Well, rest assured that no matter how strange this sounds, I am very serious about hiring you."

"All right," I said, accepting her assurance. "What's the job?"

"I'd like you to follow my husband for the period of one week," she said, hesitating before adding, "to find out if he is cheating on his diet."

"Uh, cheating on his diet."

"Yes."

"Well," I said, "that certainly is, uh, strange."

"I'm serious."

"I'm sure you are, Mrs. Randolph," I said, "but could I ask why?"

"Is that necessary for you to know in order to do the job?"

"Uh, well no, not really, but—"

"I'd rather not say, then," she said, cutting me off. "I'll pay the standard rate . . ." she added, producing a checkbook and looking at me questioningly.

"Uh, that'd be two hundred dollars a day and expenses."

"Very well," she said, pressing what appeared to be a gold pen to the top check. "Will two days be enough of a retainer?"

"That'll be fine," I said, "but do you think I could get something in, uh, cash?"

"Cash?" she asked, looking at me with a puzzled expression. "I assure you, Mr. Delvecchio, my check is quite good. I usually conduct my business affairs with checks."

"Oh, I don't doubt that, Mrs. Randolph, it's just that, uh—"

She assumed what I'm sure she thought was an understanding expression and asked, "Did you forget your wallet, Mr. Delvecchio?"

"Not really," I said, and then wished I'd said yes. I sighed and went on to tell her what had happened on the train.

"One black boy with a knife took your wallet?" she asked, staring at me.

"He wasn't really a boy—"

"Mr. Delvecchio," she said, putting her pen down before she had signed the check, "perhaps I've hired the wrong man for this job."

"Why?" I asked. "Do you expect me to beat your husband up if I catch him cheating?"

Looking annoyed she said, "No, of course not . . . but I see your point." She signed the check, tore it out and handed it to me. "Of course, I'll want an itemized bill."

Taking it I said, "I assume your husband is not at home now?"

"No, he's at work."

"Does he drive or take the subway?"

"He drives a green Monte Carlo."

"Would you like me to pick him up there, or would it be all right to start tomorrow from here?"

"Tomorrow would be fine," she said. "That's when his diet starts."

"The diet goes on for only one week?"

27

"No, of course not," she said, "but if he lasts that long I'm sure he'll make it all the way. I only need you for the one week. As soon as he cheats—if he cheats—I want you to report to me immediately."

"All right," I said, standing up. When I didn't make for the door she reached into her purse and came out with some change.

"Would ninety cents for the subway be all right?"

"Uh, if you don't mind I've had my fill of the subway for the year. I'd much rather take a cab."

She studied me for a moment, then reached into her purse again and came out with a twenty.

"Would you like to use the phone to call a cab?"

"That won't be necessary," I said. "There's a car service right next to the subway stop."

"Oh, you noticed."

I gave her my best reproachful look and said, "I'm a detective, Mrs. Randolph. I'm trained to notice things."

I left before she could ask me why I didn't notice the black kid until he was right in front of me.

I picked Randolph up in front of his house and followed him for the week. I went to lunch with him and, when his business required him to go to dinner with clients, I was there, as well. The man never so much as cheated by stealing a french fry from someone else's plate. As far as his diet was concerned, he walked the straight and narrow.

As far as his marriage was concerned, however, it was a different story.

Randolph went home late five of the seven days I followed him. On two of those nights he had dinner with a client of his investment firm in downtown Manhattan—One Liberty Plaza, to be exact, in the shade of the twin towers. The other three nights, however, he drove back to Brooklyn to a small house in the Marine Park Section and enjoyed dinner and much more with a thirtyish blonde who lived there. She was no great catch as far as I could see, but then he was a few pounds towards portly himself. As fastidious as he had been about his diet I doubted that he cheated on it while inside this house, but I knew he was cheating on his wife. It was written all over the embrace he and the woman shared in the doorway just before he left each of those nights and went back to Canarsie.

Back in my office at the end of the week I had a decision to make. I could safely report to my client that after six days her hubby had not cheated on his diet even once, bill her, collect my fee and be satisfied that I had done what I was hired for. Beyond that, however, it was a matter of ethics. I knew her husband was cheating on her, but was I bound by ethics to tell her?

Was I ever bound by ethics before? I had always done what I thought was right for me. That's what had helped me to end up a P.I. instead of Police Commissioner. While on patrol one night I'd been attacked and beaten up pretty badly. In the hospital I made up my mind that I'd never take a beating like that again, from anyone. The next guy who tried it ended up dead and I ended up in hot water because he'd had a father who knew some people who knew some people. . . .

The deal had been a pension for me, and a P.I. ticket. Either that, or a prison sentence if I fought it. All it had cost me was my "career," and I'd been doing what was right for me ever since.

I'd had a case not long ago, however, where my client had ended up killing his wife because I'd found out what he hired me to find out and told him. His wife and her lover had stolen something from him with intentions of selling it back. I got it

29

back, told him the story, and a week later his wife and her boyfriend were dead and I had a check for five thousand dollars for "services."

I tore the check up and turned him in. Had that been ethics? No, I just hadn't liked him thinking he could pay me off to keep my mouth shut about murder.

This wasn't murder, though. This was a cheating husband, and apparently his wife had no idea—or had she? Had she really hired me to see if he was cheating on his diet? Or had she been too proud to hire me to see if he was cheating on her, figuring that if I found out I'd tell her, anyway?

Now the question was, should I?

I took the question across the hall to my neighbor, Samantha Karson. Samantha was a pretty blonde who made her living—such as it was—as a writer. She wrote historical romance novels under the name "Kit Karson"—although you'd think it would be the other way around. Anyway, she had aspirations towards bigger things, which was why she had changed the name a bit. To date she'd published three novels and about a half a dozen short stories in the romance field, but she always felt that my occupation might be fodder for that something else, so we talked a lot. Sometimes we did more than talk when one or both of us got lonely, but we were good friends and not much more.

What more is there?

I knocked on her door and showed her the container of Chinese food I'd bought down the block, and she invited me in to share it with her. Over beef with broccoli, pork lo mein, fried rice and ribs I told her my predicament and asked her for her opinion.

"That's a tough one, Nicky," she said. Aside from some friends from my childhood who still called me "Nicky D," she and my father were the only people who called me Nicky. Oh yeah, and nosy Mrs. Goldstein.

She licked some rib grease off her fingers and then picked up another one and bit into it.

"Thanks," I said, "I knew you'd help."

She shrugged her shoulders inside the knee-length white sweatshirt she was wearing and said, "Tell her what she hired you to tell her. Why make her miserable?"

"Wouldn't you want to know if your husband was cheating on you?"

She smiled and said, "I would know."

"Well, maybe she knows, too," I said, "and that's why she hired me to check his diet."

"I don't think so."

"Why not?"

"Because if she was figuring you to find out anyway then what's there to hide? She might as well come out and hire you to find out without playing games."

"Then what the hell did she have me checking his diet for?"

"Maybe she really wants him to lose weight."

"Everybody wants to lose weight."

She was in the act of picking up a rib and seemed to take that remark personally.

"Except you, my love," I said quickly. "You're perfect the way you are."

She smiled, said, "Thanks," and picked up the rib.

As if to put off the decision of whether or not to tell Mrs. Randolph about her husband's indiscretion, I decided to follow Mr. Randolph one more day, to give it the full week.

His routine that day was similar to that of the previous days, and he ended up at that house in Marine Park. After he

31

had let himself in with his key I parked down the block with a view of the house and settled down for the wait I had become used to when suddenly the front door opened again and he came out—running. He ran to his car, got in, gunned the engine to life and took off.

I sat still for a few moments. It wasn't really necessary to follow him. Where else could he be going but home? Whatever had happened in that house in the past few minutes had sent him running, and I was curious about what it was.

Curious, but not crazy.

I had seen enough "Rockford Files" and "Harry O" to know what I'd find if I went into that house now. Besides the fact that I'd have to break in illegally, I just knew that if I did go in there I was going to find a body, probably of the woman who lived there. If I didn't go in, then I wouldn't find it, and maybe she wouldn't be dead.

How's that for logic?

For her sake and mine I started my own engine and went home.

"You just left?" Sam asked in disbelief.

"That's right."

She had come over as soon as she heard me get home, to find out what I had decided to do.

"Weren't you curious?"

"Sure I was."

"Then how could you just leave?" she demanded. "He could have killed her, you know? She could be dead."

"First of all, he didn't have time to kill her," I said. "He was in and out in a couple of minutes, maybe less. Secondly, she doesn't have to be dead. They could have had a big fight—"

"In a couple of minutes?"

"Well, you just said he could have killed her in a couple of minutes. Why couldn't they have had a fight?"

"I don't understand why you didn't go into the house."

"Because I have a license to protect, Sam," I explained, "I can't go breaking into people's houses. This is not 'Riptide,' this is real."

"So, how will you find out what happened?"

"If they did have a fight he won't go back there this week," I reasoned.

"Especially if he killed her," she said in her best smart-aleck tone.

"If she's dead," I said, very distinctly, "it'll be in tomorrow's papers."

"You know what you're doing?"

"What?"

"You're waiting for your problem to resolve itself," she accused. "If they had a fight and broke up, you don't have to tell his wife he's been cheating, and if she's dead it comes out the same way. Either way, you can collect your fee with a clear conscience."

"Except for one thing."

"What's that?"

"If she is dead, it *is* possible that he killed her," I admitted, uncomfortably.

"Well, if that's the case, then you've got a whole new problem, my friend."

She turned to leave and I said, "Where are you going?"

"I left Lance and Desiree in a clinch," she said, referring to one of her romance novels.

As she left I thought, I wish I had left Mr. Randolph and his lady in one.

The next day it was in the papers, the *Post* and the *Daily*

33

News. A woman was found murdered—strangled—in her house in Marine Park. Her name was being withheld until her family could be notified. The police were seeking a mysterious male friend who had been visiting her regularly, and expected to make an arrest shortly.

I had the papers spread out on my desk and was wondering what I should do about it when there was a knock on the office door. At first I figured it was Sam coming to gloat, but she would have knocked on the apartment door.

The knocking became a banging and I circled my desk, calling out, "Coming!"

I opened the door expecting a potential client and instead looked down at Detective Vito Matucci. Behind him was his partner, Detective Weinstock.

"Well, well," I said, looking down at him, "if it isn't Detective Tom Thumb."

Matucci, all five foot six or seven of him, shook with rage and said, "I don't take that from you, scumbag!"

"Sure you do, Vito," I said. "All the time."

"We'd like to talk to you, Delvecchio," Weinstock said, trying to avoid a confrontation.

"Come on in, fellas," I said, walking away from the door to my desk. I closed the newspapers and folded my hands on top of them.

"I see you've been reading the papers," Matucci said, gesturing towards my desk.

"Actually, I was trying to housebreak my cat. Would you like me to read you the funnies, Vito?"

"Can the crap, Delvecchio," Weinstock said. "This is serious business."

"What can I do for *you,* Detective Weinstock?" I asked, making it plain that whatever it was I might do it for him, but not his partner. Matucci and I had managed to go through the

Academy together without speaking a civil word to each other, and things hadn't changed much since then.

"We got a request from the six-three precinct to check you out, Delvecchio."

"For what?"

"You read about that woman who was killed in her house in Marine Park?"

"Sure, it's all over the papers," I said, starting to sweat. I had a feeling I knew what he was going to say.

"Well, it seems that the detectives who caught the case in the six-three were told by some neighbors that a strange car had been parked on the block for the past week or so."

"Is that a fact?"

"Not every day, mind you," Weinstock said, "but enough to make it suspicious."

"And somebody took down the license plate number," Matucci added.

I knew it.

"Guess who the car checks out to?" Matucci asked with a shit-eating grin on his face.

"So?" I asked. "Is there a law against parking, now?"

"No law against it," Weinstock said, "it's just interesting that you should be parking on the same block where a woman was killed. Would you know anything about that, Delvecchio?"

"Not really."

"I say different," Matucci said.

"What you say, Vito, is a matter of no importance to me or anybody with half a brain."

Weinstock jumped in before Vito could come back at me. "You *were* there, weren't you?"

"Do these neighbors say I was parked in front of the dead woman's house?"

"No," Weinstock admitted, "down the block, but you could see the dead woman's house from there."

"Which one was it?" I asked. "The papers didn't give the address."

"If you don't know we ain't telling you," Matucci said.

"Fine."

"What were you doing there, Delvecchio?" Weinstock asked.

"I was tailing a wayward husband, Weinstock."

"What's his name?"

"I can't tell you that—"

"You have no right to withhold the name of your client, Delvecchio."

"No legal right, I know. I'd like to talk to my client, though, and clear it with them so I don't end up going to court to get my fee. Clients take a dim view when you get them involved with the cops, Weinstock. All of a sudden they don't want to pay you, you know?"

"All right, look," Weinstock said, "I'm gonna give you the name of the detective in the six-three. He wants to talk to you. I told him you'd cooperate."

"That was kind of you."

"Just don't make me out a liar, huh?" he asked. "Talk to your client, and then go and talk to Detective Walters in the six-three. I'll leave it to him to light a fire under your ass if you decide to clam up. Fair?"

"Fair."

"Wait a minute," Matucci said. "We can sweat this bum—"

"It's not our case, Vito," Weinstock said. "Let's go. We've got work to do."

"But—" Matucci said, but Weinstock was already out the door.

"Have a nice day," I said to Matucci. He took a few seconds to think up a good comeback, then gave up and left in a huff, slamming the door behind him.

Technically speaking, I had no proof that the woman in the papers was the woman Randolph had been visiting. Once I satisfied myself that she was, I'd go and talk to Detective Walters.

I left my office and drove over the Brooklyn Bridge. I wanted to be at Randolph's office when he got there.

Of course, there was the chance that he wouldn't show up that morning, but that wouldn't look good if his wife or the cops looked closely at his movements.

He showed up at his regular time of eight forty-five, and I was waiting outside the building for him.

"Mr. Randolph?" I said, calling out to him as he approached the revolving door.

He stopped short and backed up a step, as if he thought I might be a street panhandler or worse.

"I'd like to talk to you, Mr. Randolph. My name is Nick Delvecchio."

"What do you want?"

"I'm the private investigator working for your wife."

"My wife?" he asked. "A p-private investigator?"

I nodded.

"I've been following you for a week."

The enormity of that statement struck him immediately.

"Can we talk in your office?"

"No—" he said quickly.

"It would be more private."

"Oh—yes, of course. C-come upstairs."

I followed him up to his office, where he barreled through the reception area without returning one of four different greetings. We entered his office which, unlike many of the others, was not just a glassed in cubicle, but an honest to goodness, four wall room. He wasn't the boss, but he must have been pretty close.

"Mr. Randolph," I said as he sank into the chair behind the desk with a stricken look, "I'm not here to make your life difficult."

"Why would my wife hire a detective?"

"The reason seemed pretty silly to me at the time, but apparently she was worried that you might be cheating on your diet."

"My diet?" he asked, staring at me incredulously. He started to laugh then, an ironic, almost hysterical laughter that I was afraid he would lose control of.

"My diet," he said, shaking his head as the laughter wound down. "I have a c-company physical coming up soon. A promotion could hang in the balance. That would mean more money. Myra would be worried about that."

"Needless to say, I followed you several times to Marine Park—including yesterday."

He stayed silent then, staring into space.

"You were only in the house a couple of minutes, Mr. Randolph. I don't think you killed her. I think she was dead when you got there, and you panicked and ran."

"Mary—" he began, shaking his head, then stopped short. "Do you intend to blackmail me?"

I shook my head irritably and said, "No, that's not why I'm here."

"Have you—told my wife anything?"

"Your wife hired me to check on your diet, Mr. Randolph, not to check on your fidelity. To be honest, I've been wrestling with myself as to whether or not I should tell her . . . but I honestly think that you should."

"I—can't—"

"And you'll have to talk to the police," I added. "I'll back your story that you were only in the house for a couple of minutes. That won't look too bad for you, believe me."

"I—"

"I'm giving you my expert advice, Mr. Randolph," I said, trying again. "Get yourself a lawyer, talk to the cops and your wife."

Randolph looked at me and asked, "How much time do I have?"

"Not much," I said. "The police have already talked to me. I didn't say anything, but I've got a license to protect." I stood up and added, "I'll have to talk to them today. I don't have much of a choice."

I didn't apologize to him because I was doing him a favor, and I didn't have to, but his wife was my client, and I didn't want to see him railroaded simply because he panicked.

Ethics are ethics, but a person has got to eat, too. After I left Randolph's office I drove to Canarsie. I wanted to give my report to Mrs. Randolph about her husband's diet and collect my fee before things got muddled.

"Mr. Delvecchio," Myra Randolph said as she opened the door. "I didn't expect you."

"May I come in, Mrs. Randolph?"

"Uh, yes, of course."

She seemed nervous as she backed up to allow me to enter. I closed the door behind me and followed her into her living room.

"Are you here to report on your progress?"

"Yes. I came to tell you that throughout the week that I followed your husband he never once cheated on his diet within my eyesight."

"That's wonderful," she said, reaching for her bag. It was

then that I noticed that her purse was different from the one she'd had the first time I was there. She was wearing a chic two piece suit which matched the purse. A woman dresses with matching purse when she is going out.

"Have you prepared a bill?"

"As a matter of fact," I said, taking out the one I'd prepared that morning, "I have. My expenses are on it, as well."

"I'm sure it's in order," she said, glancing only at the bottom line and writing a check.

She handed me the check and dropped the checkbook on the chair between her purse and a copy of the *Daily News*. I folded the check and slid it into my pocket after noticing the number. She had written only one other check between this one and the one she'd given me as a retainer.

"Thank you, Mrs. Randolph."

"On the contrary, Mr. Delvecchio," she said. "Thank you."

She saw me to the door rather hurriedly, bade me good-bye, and shut it quickly. I walked to my car, got in, and sat there a few moments. During that time she came out of her house carrying two suitcases, with her purse over her shoulder, got into a green Gran Prix parked in front of the next house, and drove away.

I waited a few more moments before getting out of the car and walking up to the front door.

I know what I told Sam about protecting my license by not breaking into the house in Marine Park, but I didn't think I'd be finding a body in this house. Besides, several things about Mrs. Randolph puzzled me enough to produce my lock picks, open the front door and illegally enter my client's house.

I went over it all again in my mind during the ride to La Guardia Airport.

For a woman who had been sure to advise me that she'd

want an itemized bill, Mrs. Randolph had been very quick to look at the bottom line and write me a check for the amount without examining the bill further.

It was obvious that she'd been just about on the way out when I got there. She'd paid me off to get rid of me so she could leave for the airport. Of course, I didn't know that at the time, but I did wonder about her nervousness.

And then there was her checkbook, which had obviously been left behind by accident. It had slid down the cushion and between the pages of the newspaper, and she had simply picked up her purse and accidentally left it behind. I knew she had written one check between the two she'd given me, and since it was the second week of the month, there were no monthly bills to be paid. (I hadn't thought of charge cards, where the bills come due at odd dates, but then if I had, I might not have gone into the house.)

Anyway, that other check had been made out to a Mary Burgess, and had then been voided. It had been dated the day before, the same day Alex Randolph's "Mary" had been murdered.

Of course, there was nothing concrete in all of that, but enough to make me suspicious enough to call the six-three and relay it to Detective Walters. I was hoping that just the fact that the wife of a murder suspect might be leaving town would be enough for him to send a car to the airport to stop her.

I was wrong.

"Look, Delvecchio," he said on the phone, "call me if you see *Mister* Randolph leaving. His wife is free to go."

"But Walters—"

"I've got to go. I've got cases up the ass to work on."

I'd shouted into the phone, but he'd hung up.

Now I was driving like a maniac to La Guardia Airport in

Queens, hoping that I'd arrive before her plane left—whichever plane that was.

I parked in the long-term parking and took the elevator to the bridge between the indoor lot and the terminal.

La Guardia's different from New York's other major airport, Kennedy, in that all the terminals are connected in one big, semi-circular building, rather than each airline having their own building.

That would make it easier, if "easy" was a word to use. With as many major airlines as there were, how was I supposed to pick one out?

I began walking through the halls, stopping at each airline's ticket terminal to check the lines, and the monitors for the outgoing flights.

All I could figure was that since she was in such a hurry to leave, her plane had to be leaving soon. I also limited myself to major airlines, figuring that she would have been able to get a ticket on a flight at short notice.

There were three flights leaving within the half hour: Eastern to Florida, United to California, and American to Chicago. I made a mental note of the gates, and started with the Florida flight.

I had to stop at the metal detectors, and damned if I wasn't wearing my big western belt, the one that always makes the damned things go off. I had to take it off, hand it to a guard, walk through and reclaim the belt. I checked the gate for the Eastern flight to Florida, and she wasn't there. I checked with the ground attendants, and they checked their computer to see if she was confirmed on their flight. She wasn't.

I had to go through the same thing to get to the United gate, and had been dumb enough to loop the belt back on. Take it off, hand it to the guard, go through and run to the gate. I got there just as they were starting to board. This time

I got smart. I had the ground attendant check her computer for her flight, then asked her if she could simply put the name in and check for all outgoing flights.

"I'm sorry, sir, but you would need a flight number in order for us to check it for you."

"Okay, thanks."

I thought I'd gotten smart, but now I had to run to catch the Chicago flight.

As I came within sight of the metal detector she was just about to go through it.

"Mrs. Randolph!" I called out.

She turned at the sound of my voice, frowning, and then recognized me. I had no proof of anything and she could have brazened it out, but instead she panicked. She pushed the woman in front of her aside and ran through the metal detector.

It started beeping like crazy and one of the guards called after her. It was still beeping when I ran through it with my belt.

"Hey!" the female guard yelled at me, too, but I kept running.

Actually, if I had stopped to think about it she wasn't going anywhere. They wouldn't have let the flight take off until she had been checked out, anyway, but neither one of us was doing any thinking at the moment. I didn't know at that moment what she had in her bag, and I still don't know how she expected to get it through the detector, unless she had simply forgotten all about it. After all, she did have a lot on her mind. . . .

As she reached the gate for her flight they were calling for first class passengers to board.

"Mrs. Randolph!" I shouted, trying to keep her from rushing into the boarding tunnel.

She turned and when she saw me she started reaching into her purse. I started for her like an idiot and couldn't believe it when she came out of her bag with a gun.

"Stay away!" she shouted.

"No, Mrs. Randolph, don't shoot!" The panic in my voice was apparent, even to me. Anyone who tells you they can look down the barrel of a gun *without* panicking is a fucking liar. I know, I've looked down the barrel at death before. The last time I ended up taking a beating that almost killed me, and I swore that would never happen again. If I'd had a gun on me right then I would have gladly shot her. Since I didn't have a gun I was going to have to try and talk to her before I rushed her . . .

Suddenly people started shouting and screaming, and then they started to run for cover. Several of them passed between us and before I could say anything to her she suddenly turned and ran into the passageway.

"Jesus," I muttered, taking off after her. If she got onto the plane with passengers already on it, we'd have a situation here that I certainly wasn't equipped to handle—and one that I probably would have to take the blame for causing.

I ran through the doorway into the passageway, shouting to the attendant, "Call ahead and have them shut the door."

Please, I thought, make it a long passageway.

I saw her ahead of me, running unsteadily on high heels, which slowed her progress. By the time she reached the door of the plane it was swinging shut in front of her. When she saw that I heard her scream, "No!" and then she whirled on me with the gun extended.

My heart began to pound. I had absolutely nowhere to go, and steeled myself to rush her. I had to hope she was nervous enough to miss her first shot.

"Put the gun down, Mrs. Randolph," a voice shouted from behind me.

I turned and saw Detective Walters, flanked by two airport security men who had their guns drawn and trained on my client.

"I didn't mean to kill her," she shouted as I turned back to her. I stood very still, afraid that if I moved she'd pull the trigger. Let the experts handle it.

"We know, Mrs. Randolph, but if you kill Delvecchio, or any of us, that will be deliberate murder. You don't want to do that."

She hesitated a moment, then the gun began to waver and she said through tears, "No, I don't want to do that . . ."

Walters moved roughly past me and I didn't move until he had her gun in his hand.

Mrs. Randolph, being an amateur murderer, had made several mistakes. She had used her own car, she had written that check so that the dead woman's name was in her checkbook, and she had finally panicked when the enormity of her deed struck her, and tried to leave town.

After hanging up on me Detective Walters had gotten a report from some men he had asked questions in the Marine Park neighborhood. One of them had come up with a description of Mrs. Randolph's car, and a partial plate. That had been enough to send him to La Guardia, where he heard someone talking about a crazy man running through the airport.

Walters said that Mrs. Randolph had obviously intended to buy the girl off, and when she wouldn't be bought, had strangled her in anger. (Why she didn't shoot her, no one knew. If she'd had the gun in the airport, why hadn't she taken it with her to see the girl? Mrs. Randolph wasn't talking, on advice from her attorney.)

Me, I think she planned it. I also think she planned for me to be a witness against her husband, which was why she'd put me on his tail in the first place—even though he really did have a company physical coming up. (Sam said if she'd planned it, why did she write the check? I still can't answer that one.)

Oh yeah, the cops got an anonymous phone call telling them to go to the house in Marine Park, where they might find a body—and would certainly have been able to find plenty of Alex Randolph's fingerprints, if not some belongings.

The call had come from a woman.

Of course, the matter of ethics still existed but after all, I had given my client what she had hired me for, and collected my fee.

Still, Sam might have been right. Maybe I stalled long enough for the situation to resolve itself, but then I think about what might have happened if I hadn't tailed Randolph that one last day.

The Vanishing Virgin

1

"One of my virgins has vanished," the man sitting across the table said.

I frowned at him. I'd heard of men collecting women before—harems, and all that—but virgins? What would one do with them?

"Perhaps I'd better explain," George Vanguard said.

"It would be appreciated."

I didn't usually talk like that, but there was something about Vanguard that brought it out in me.

He had called me earlier and asked for an appointment; I lied and told him that he was in luck, I'd had a cancellation. His name was George Vanguard and he was a playwright with a problem.

"You see," he began, "in my new play—which is now in rehearsals, by the way—the three central characters are virgins."

In this day and age? "Is it a fantasy?"

"How did you know?" he replied, looking at me with surprise and something akin to respect. It never hurts to impress a potential client early.

"I guessed. Go on, please."

"Yes, well, the girl who plays one of the virgins hasn't shown up for rehearsal in two days. It's wreaking havoc with my schedule, as I'm sure you can imagine."

The guy came off like a daisy, but I wanted to give him the benefit of the doubt—which was kind of hard to do with a fellow who wears a pink shirt and lavender jacket with matching kerchief.

"Indeed," I said.

"Well, that's it," he said, shrugging. "We simply cannot find her," he added, for dramatic effect.

"Have you tried her home?"

"Well, we've *called*, of course."

"You haven't gone to her place to check?"

"I simply don't have the *time*," he explained. "We're running rehearsals around her, but we can't do that *forever*. I'd like to hire you to find her within the next two days."

"Why the time limit?"

"Well, I don't *want* to replace her, she's *perfect* for the part, but in a few days that will be a moot point. I will simply be *forced* to replace her and continue rehearsals. We open next month, you know."

"On Broadway?"

"Off Broadway," he said, as if he were implying *who wants to be on Broadway?*

"I see. Do you have her address with you?"

"Well, of *course*," he scolded. His nose wrinkled when he scolded. I decided he was definitely gay—that's why I'm a *detective*.

He rattled off her address and I wrote it down on the doodle pad I carry in my pocket. It was in Manhattan, and *I* wrinkled *my* nose at the prospect of going across the bridge.

"My fee," I told him, "is twenty dollars an hour, plus expenses."

"My backers will pay it."

"I'll need a retainer," I said, firmly.

He wrinkled his nose and took out a checkbook. He signed

with a flourish of loops and circles. It was a lavender check for three hundred and twenty dollars. Sixteen hours' work. I wondered if he expected those hours to be spread over two days. I've been known to work on a case like this for four hours a day, or even two, in which case it stretched out. It depended on whether or not I had other cases.

Which, at the moment, I did not.

Accepting the check I asked, "What about her friends?"

"What about them?"

"Who are they?"

"How should I know that? I don't socialize with the girl, for heaven's sake," he said, as if the very thought of socializing with a *woman* was appalling. "As for the other girls in the show, you can come to the theater and I'll introduce you."

"Where are you rehearsing?"

He wrinkled his nose again.

"We simply could not get a theater in Manhattan, so we're using an old movie theater in Bay Ridge. Do you know where Bay Ridge is?"

"I can find it," I said, with my tongue in my cheek.

He gave me the address, a small theater on Third Avenue.

"When will you come down?"

"Are you rehearsing today?"

"Well, of *course*. That's where I should be *now*."

I checked my watch. Twelve-forty.

"After I check out the girl's apartment I'll come right over. What's her name, by the way?"

"Oh, of course," he said, almost simpering, "how silly of us. Her name is Amy Butterworth."

"What does she look like?"

"Oh, I'm terrible at describing *women*. I can do men much more easily."

I believed him.

49

I smiled and said, "Give it your best shot."

"Let me see," he said, looking at the ceiling. "She's about twenty-two, built rather petitely except for her breasts, which are rather large for a girl her size. She's just right for the part, you know, virginal, but with a touch of wanton, do you know what I mean?"

"I believe so."

"She has blond hair, long," he said, touching his shoulders, "blue eyes, and she laughs a lot. Does that help?"

"It'll do. I'll probably drop by the theater somewhere around three, after I've been to her place and talked to the police."

"The police?" he said, alarmed. "Oh dear, we shouldn't have any bad publicity."

"I'm just going to check with them and see if she's . . . turned up, anywhere, like in a hospital."

"Oh, I see. That makes sense."

"Thank you."

He rose and extended his hand for me to shake. I had already done that when he arrived, and I dreaded doing it again. He was tall, about six-one, but very thin, like a blade of pink-and-lavender grass. His eyes were a pale gray and slightly watery and he seemed as if he'd be the nervous type even under normal circumstances. His handshake hadn't gotten any firmer since his arrival, when it had felt like a warm, moist dishrag.

"Thank you ever so much, Mr. Delvecchio," he gushed, pumping my hand. I hate men who gush. "I'm sure my cast is just going to love you, but remember—my business before your pleasure, eh?" he said, trying in his own way to be slightly bawdy—I think.

"I'll keep that in mind."

2

The girl who opened Amy Butterworth's door had long dark hair, elegantly thin red lips, and two of the biggest breasts I'd ever seen. I got a real good look at them, too, because she was wearing a thin T-shirt on which someone had stenciled the words "Fly Me." Below that she was wearing tight designer jeans, no shoes, and red nail polish on her toes.

The apartment was on West Fifty-sixth Street in Manhattan, and I'd had to walk up four flights of stairs to knock on the door. I was acutely aware of the fact that I was soaking wet from perspiration, not all of it from exertion. I was experiencing the usual heebie-jeebies from crossing the bridge from Brooklyn to "the City."

"Hello," she said, cheerfully. "Can I help you?"

"Soon as I get my breath back you can," I said.

"You'll have to do better than that before I invite a strange man into my apartment," she said, thinking it was a compliment.

"The climb," I said, panting.

"Oh."

"And this heat doesn't help, either. Why don't they air-condition these halls?"

"Are you kidding? I had to buy my own window air conditioner."

I could feel the cool air coming out of her apartment, feeling cooler yet on my wet face.

"My name is Delvecchio, Nick Delvecchio. I'm a private investigator looking for Amy Butterworth."

"Do you have some I.D.?" she asked, like a true New Yorker.

I showed it to her and she stepped back and said, "All right, come on in and cool off."

"Thank you."

I entered and she shut the door behind us. She was tall, about five-nine in her bare feet. With heels she would be taller than me.

"I'm Amy's roommate. What's this about?"

"Have you seen her lately? Over the past few days?"

"No, I haven't seen her for three or four days, but that's not unusual."

"Oh? Why not? Does she stay away for days at a time?"

"No, I'm a stew."

"Pardon?"

"A stewardess—or flight attendant, as they now call us. I haven't been in town for days. I just got back today from London. Has something happened to her?"

"I hope not. May I sit down?"

"Oh, sure, sorry, please," she said, nervously. "My name's Lucy, Lucy Mills."

"Nick Delvecchio," I said.

"Can I ask who hired you to look for Amy, and why?"

"Sure. Do you know George Vanguard?"

"The playwright?"

"Yes. He's the man who hired me. Seems Amy hasn't shown up for rehearsals for two days, and he's worried."

"About his play, I'll bet."

"That may be, but he did hire me."

"He's a fag," she said with distaste. "He probably hassled Amy and she took off for a couple of days."

"You're not worried, then?"

"No," she said, shrugging. "She's an actress, isn't she? And she's everything an actress should be: temperamental, sensitive, and a little nutty. She'll be back."

"Well, if you don't mind," I said, handing her one of the business cards I'd just had printed up. All they had on them was my name, my occupation, and home phone. "If she shows up within the next couple of days, would you give me a call?"

"I'm flying out again tomorrow night, but if she shows by then I'll call you."

"I appreciate it."

She walked me to the door and said, "When I get back why don't I check in with you again and see if you've found her. If not, you might want to talk to me again."

I wondered if it would be presumptuous of me to read something else into her offer. I figured I'd just have to wait and see.

"That'd be fine," I said, and left.

3

Before going to the theater I called a detective in Missing Persons I used to work with when I first became a cop. I asked if they had anything on an Amy Butterworth, or anyone who fit her description. Their listing was citywide, and if she'd been in a hospital or morgue in any of the boroughs, they would have known about it.

They didn't, which meant she wasn't in one of those places—or maybe just not yet.

I got to the theater a little after three and rehearsals were in full swing. I took a seat about halfway down and watched for a while, waiting for an opening. It was hot as hell in there, and obvious the air-conditioning was out of order. Still, I felt a lot better just being back in Brooklyn.

"I won't tell them why you're here," Vanguard said, sitting next to me. "You can do that individually."

"Fine."

"Until you speak to them privately, they'll probably just assume that you're another backer."

"Good enough."

"Lord, I wish they'd fix the air-conditioning in here," he bitched.

"It could be worse," I said. "We could be in Florida in July instead of New York."

"True."

A woman started up the aisle toward us and Vanguard started to get up, saying in a low tone, "Maybe I'd better introduce you to my director."

"Nick Delvecchio," he said aloud, "this is my assistant director, Sherry Logan."

"Mr. Delvecchio," she said, extending her hand as a man would.

Her grip was surprisingly firm. She was auburn-haired, with green eyes and a wide, full-lipped mouth. She reminded me very much of an actress I had seen in a private-eye movie my friend Billy Palmer had showed me, once. The film was called *P.J.*, and the actress's name was Gayle Hunnicut.

Unlike the actress, however, she was not tall—maybe five-four—and she was slim and small-breasted. Her mouth was very sensuous; the upper and lower lip were of equal fullness. A tendril of hair was plastered to her forehead by perspiration.

I placed her age at about twenty-eight, but she could have gone a couple of years in either direction with no problem. What with her job I figured her for closer to thirty than not.

"I'm pleased to meet you, Mr. Delvecchio. Are you interested in the theater?"

"Not particularly. Theater people, yes, but not the theater

itself. I have to meet a few of the people here, but perhaps we could talk later, say over dinner?"

She frowned at my abrupt offer and asked, "About what?" She was polite, because she still wasn't sure that I wasn't a backer.

"Oh, about theater people."

Her puzzled frown turned shrewd.

"Anyone in particular?"

I handed her one of my cards and said, "Amy Butterworth."

She read the card and turned to Vanguard. "Oh, George, you didn't."

"I certainly did," he replied haughtily. "Cooperate with him, Sherry. Let me introduce him around and then you can talk to him."

"If you don't mind," I added. I didn't want her to be hostile.

She looked at me, parting her full lips and tapping her front teeth with my card.

"No, I guess I don't mind. I'll wait for you, Mr. Delvecchio, but this dinner is going to cost you."

"That's okay," I said, "I'm on an expense account."

Vanguard frowned, and then led me toward the stage. He introduced me around without saying who and what I was, and I could tell by the polite reception that he'd been right about everyone assuming I was a backer.

The male lead in the play was a fairly young, tall, slim, somewhat effeminate-looking man named Harry Wilkens. His handshake was firmer than Vanguard's, but not as firm as Sherry Logan's.

The second lead was a huskier man who seemed a bit old to be second lead actor in an off-Broadway play. His name was Jack Dwyer and he studied me long enough to make me uncomfortable. I had the feeling he wasn't accepting me for what I appeared to be.

Next I met the other two virgins.

Linda Pollard was a petite blonde with light blue eyes and a small mouth, kind of like Lana Turner when she was real young. She was extremely slim and delicate looking and—if her breasts hadn't been so small—she could have fit Amy Butterworth's description.

The other virgin was quite different; probably, I figured, by design. Her name was Onaly O'Toole, and I had to have that repeated to me before I understood that it was her stage name.

"I was an on-aly child," she said, as if she'd been explaining it for years.

She had the blackest hair I've ever seen, worn long and parted in the center. She was tall, about five-eight, and had an arresting face. Her eyes were brown and set just a bit too far apart. Her nose was too big, but not so much so that it would hamper her career any. She was as full-breasted as Linda Pollard was petite. *Virgin* was the last word that would come to mind to describe Onaly O'Toole.

It was obvious that this was not a dress rehearsal, as virtually all of these people were wearing T-shirts and jeans.

"Those are our lead players," Vanguard said after the intros had been made. "Now that they've met you they won't question your presence in the theater. You can talk to them now or at your convenience, just please keep in mind that there is a time limit. This is Wednesday. If you can't find Amy in time for Saturday rehearsal, I'm going to have to replace her."

"I understand."

He stepped away into the center of the stage and clapped his hands, reminding me very much of a teacher I'd had in the third grade. Thinking back, I could swear that he'd been gay, too.

I became aware of a presence behind me at that point and turned to find Sherry Logan.

"I don't mind an early dinner," she said.

"Doesn't he . . ."

"George can handle this himself. Besides, I want to talk about Amy."

"Why?"

"I want this show to go on without a hitch," she said. "It's important to me. Helping you find Amy can accomplish that."

"All right," I said, "an early dinner, it is."

4

She took me to a restaurant in the area—an air-conditioned restaurant—and after we ordered a couple of iced teas she said, "So tell me how I can help you?"

"Do you know Amy well?"

"Not very well. We've worked together once or twice before, but we're not what you'd call friends."

"Had she ever done a disappearing act any of those other times you worked with her?"

"Let me think." The waitress brought our drinks. "I'm sure she missed a rehearsal or two on occasion, but I wouldn't say it was a habit with her."

"Do you know any of her hangouts?"

"Only the usual theater places," she said, mentioning a few. "Some of the others might know something more specific."

"Who are her friends in the show? Who is she close to?"

"Linda," she said, without hesitation. "Linda and Amy are very close."

"I think you're trying to tell me something without telling me something," I said.

She smiled and said, "You really are a detective."

"Are you telling me that Linda and Amy were an item?"

"Well, it's pretty common knowledge that Linda and Amy were—are—lovers."

"You're sure of that?"

"They don't flaunt it, but yes, I'm sure."

"Is Vanguard aware of this?"

"Georgie is only aware of his performers as performers, not as people."

"Well then, I guess my next step is to talk to Linda."

"Take it easy on her, Nick," she said, using my first name very easily. "She's very young, and she's as fragile as she appears to be."

"Isn't that a hazard in your business?"

"Yes," she said, as our dinner arrived.

We talked about other things: my former profession as a cop, and hers as an actress, before she decided to "switch sides," as she put it. This was actually her first chance to direct on her own—although it hardly seemed that way to me. She said that Vanguard was taking a big chance with her.

"It'll keep his budget down," she explained, being realistic. She seemed to have both feet firmly planted on the ground, and I liked that about her.

"As producer and author, Georgie will always be around with his two cents anyway, but I really am grateful for the opportunity he's given me."

"I wish you luck."

"Thank you."

"Can you tell me anything about the other people in the show?"

"Personal things, you mean?"

"That's what I mean, all right. What about Harry Wilkens? Is he involved with anyone? Or Onaly O'Toole?"

"Isn't that a great name?" she asked. "Her real name's Ann, but Onaly is a wonderful stage name." She shook her head and got back to my question. "Onaly keeps to herself, so I can't help you there—but Harry?" she said, smiling. "Georgie and Harry are *very, very* close."

"I see."

"Jack is this guy from the Midwest who was recommended to Georgie. I don't know much about him."

"I'll just have to ask him, then."

"There's only one thing I do know about him for sure."

"What's that?"

"He's not gay. He's been after me since we first met."

"Has he caught you?"

"Can I tell you anything else?"

"Yes," I said, "tell me about this play."

5

I got Linda's address from Sherry and decided to go and see her after our early dinner. The fact that Sherry insisted she go straight home—where her work awaited—certainly had a bearing on my decision.

"I'll see you tomorrow at the theater," she said, and we went our separate ways.

It was after six, but the heat was persisting.

Linda Pollard lived in an apartment on the Upper East Side of Manhattan, one that she should have had trouble paying for if she did not have a roommate, a rich daddy, or a sugar daddy. From what Sherry had told me about Amy and Linda, though, the latter seemed remote.

When she answered the door I had to explain who I was before she recognized me.

"I'm sorry," she said, frowning, "but what are you doing here?"

"I'd like to come in and talk to you, if I may."

Her eyes widened and she said, "I'm sorry, mister . . . ?"

"Delvecchio."

"I'm sorry, but maybe one of the other girls would—I mean, I don't—"

"You don't understand. I want to talk to you about Amy."

"Do you know Amy?" she asked. "Do you know where she is?" Her tone was desperate.

"No, but I'm looking for her." I took out my I.D. and showed it to her. "Vanguard hired me to try and find her."

"A private detective," she said, frowning at the card.

"May I come in?" I asked again, and this time she nodded and backed away from the door.

"Miss Pollard—"

"Linda, please."

"Linda . . . when was the last time you saw Amy?"

"We went shopping together three days ago."

"Where?"

"Oh, Fifth Avenue, Thirty-fourth Street, like that. Amy doesn't have any money, but I get some from . . . from home, so we shopped and I bought her something."

"And after that?"

"We had dinner, and then we went home. We had an early call the next morning."

"When you say you went home, does that mean . . ."

"She went to her apartment, and I came here."

"I see."

"She didn't show up the next day, or yesterday. I'm real worried. She really wanted this part. She wouldn't walk away from it, Mr. Delvecchio, not willingly."

I started to say "I see" again, but stopped myself and just nodded.

"Was anyone bothering her lately?"

"Georgie was yelling at her, but he does that sometimes."

"No, I mean were there any men following her, or calling her?"

"No, not that she mentioned."

"Would she have mentioned it to you?"

"Oh, definitely, either to me or Lucy. That's her room-mate."

"I've met her." I hadn't asked her that question, though. It was as good a reason to go back as any.

"Amy didn't talk about leaving town?"

"She'd never leave, Mr. Delvecchio—"

"Nick."

"She wants to be an actress so much. This part meant everything to her."

This time I did say "I see," and immediately grimaced.

"Is there somewhere she would go if something was bothering her?"

"If something was bothering her, she'd come to me . . . Nick."

I stood and said, "Well, thank you for your help, Miss— Linda."

"If you find her, you'll let me know?"

"Yes, and if you hear from her, call me at this number," I said, giving her one of my cards. "Oh, by the way. Does she have any family in town?"

"She has no family anywhere, Nick. Neither of us do. That's why we became such good friends."

I nodded and said, "Thanks, Linda."

"Please," she said, grabbing my arm, "find her."

"I'm going to do my best."

I went home from Linda Pollard's apartment and ran into Sam in front of the building. Sam is Samantha Karson, my neighbor across the hall. She's a romance writer who uses the name "Kit" Karson on her books. A pale blonde who reminds me of a prettier Sissy Spacek, she invited me to have a drink with her, and I accepted. We went to a place that had opened up nearby called the Can-U-Drop-Inn and sat at the bar.

"What do you know about the theater?" I asked her.

"Nothing."

"Big help."

"I try," she said.

I told her about the case and she listened quietly. She was real good at listening. She wanted to break into the mystery field, and she saw me as the source of her plots.

I finished my beer and climbed down off my stool.

"Going?"

I nodded. "I'm wiped. This heat wrings me out."

"Working tonight?" she asked.

I shook my head. "I'll go back to the theater in the morning and talk to everyone. There's no point in pussy-footing around this thing. If any of them know where she is, they'll tell me. If they don't, it'll hold up the show."

"Good luck. I'm going to have another drink and get to know the bartender."

"Why?" I asked. "This place will be closed in a month."

She shrugged and said, "I need a couple of drinks before I get to work tonight."

Sam did most of her writing at night. Sometimes, if I listen real hard, I can hear her typewriter going at three in the morning.

"Okay," I said. "I'll see you sometime tomorrow."

"I'll be in after three."

I nodded, shook hands, and went out into the waning heat. By eight or nine o'clock, maybe it would even be down to eighty.

6

The next morning I had breakfast and headed for the theater. When I got there, all the doors were open and the people inside were complaining.

"Not only is it the heat," someone up on the stage was yelling, "but now we've got this smell."

Vanguard called back petulantly, "I've opened the windows and doors. What more do you want?"

"Get somebody in here to find out what that smell is." I saw now that it was Onaly O'Toole who was complaining.

"Onaly—"

"God," she said, "it smells like something curled up in a corner and died."

I was halfway down the aisle now and the smell hit me. I stopped short, took a wary breath, and my stomach sank.

"George," I said.

He turned and saw me, waved a hand for me to wait.

"Vanguard!" I said, moving to him and grabbing his arm.

"What is it?"

"Get everyone out of here."

"What?"

"Out!" I said. "Get everyone out . . . now!"

"Why?"

"Take a deep breath, George."

He did and said, "I smell it, for heaven's sake; what can I do—"

"Get everyone out and I'll find out what the smell is. If it's what I think it is . . ." Actually, I knew what it was because I'd smelled it plenty of times when I was a cop.

"Oh my Lord," he said, his eyes widening.

"Exactly. Now come on, get everyone outside."

"All right, people," he shouted, "take five. Everyone outside."

The complaints started, but he was doing a good job of herding them out. As he passed me on his own way out I stopped him again.

"George, who's not here?"

"Uh, Dwyer, Jack Dwyer. He's not here yet, but I assumed he was just late."

"Where's the smell coming from?"

"There's a stairway backstage—stage right—that goes downstairs. It seems to be coming from there."

"What's down there?"

"It's used for storage."

"Okay. Go outside and wait for me."

He nodded and turned away, and I heard him say, "Linda, come on, love; let's go outside. You don't want to stay in here . . ."

". . . looking for my purse . . ."

The rest of what they were saying got lost as I made my way to the stage. I hopped up and went backstage. I made like Snagglepuss—"Exit, staaage right!"—and found the stairway.

He was right. The smell was stronger here, and was rising.

I went downstairs, breathing as shallowly as possible. I knew that a civilian would be choking by now. I found myself in a small hallway with two doors on the right and one on the left, directly under the stage.

I checked the two on the right and found small storage rooms. The smell was no stronger in either of them. That left the door under the stage.

When I opened it I was hit first by a wave of air that might have been coming from a furnace, and then by the smell. I took out my handkerchief, held it over my mouth, and went inside.

I found her fairly easily. Someone had piled debris on top of her, but the smell and insect activity led me right to her.

Whoever had killed her and put her down there had probably figured to come back eventually and move her. What they hadn't counted on was the air-conditioning going on the fritz. Amy—if it was Amy, and I felt sure it was—had swelled up like a balloon and done what a balloon does when it's filled too much. She was as ripe as they come.

When I was on the job and we were called to the scene of a D.O.A. what we usually did was drop a handful of coffee into a frying pan. In moments the strong smell of burning coffee would help dilute the odor of the corpse. I knew some cops who could eat their lunch in the same room while waiting for the M.E. and never miss a swallow. I wasn't one of them.

I turned to leave and saw her in the doorway.

"Linda," I said.

"My God," she said, "it smells terrible."

"Didn't expect that, did you?" I asked.

She had one hand over her mouth. In her other was a .22 caliber revolver.

"Where did you get the gun, Linda?"

"My father gave it to me when I told him I was moving to New York. I carry it with me everywhere."

"And how did you come to use it on Amy?"

"We had a fight."

"Over . . . someone else?"

"I see you've heard the stories," she said, bitterly. "Amy and I weren't lovers. In fact, we were hardly even friends. We just had a lot in common."

"What changed that?"

"When she got the role as the first virgin, and I got the role as the third."

"And the second?"

"Onaly."

"What happened between you and Amy?"

"She got uppity when she landed the role of first virgin. That night we stayed to go over some lines, and we got into a fight. She said I was third virgin because I had third-virgin talent."

"That wasn't fair."

"No, it wasn't. I told her I could very easily be second virgin. She sneered and said the only way I could do that was if Onaly died."

"And you showed her different, didn't you?"

"That's right, I did," Linda Pollard said. "I showed her that I could move up by her dying."

"And how would you have moved up to first virgin, Linda? By killing Onaly?"

"I wouldn't kill Onaly," she said, staring at me strangely. "She's a nice girl."

"And Amy wasn't."

"No," Linda Pollard said. "She was a snot."

"Did you drag her down here by yourself?"

"I dragged her to the stairs and pushed her down, then

pulled her in here and covered her. I didn't know where else to put her!"

Her eyes were tearing now from the smell, as mine were. I was so wet from perspiration that I felt as if I were standing in a pool.

"Come on, Linda. Let's go upstairs."

"No," she said, choking a bit, "you'll tell them."

"I'll have to."

"No!"

"Are you going to kill me, too?" I asked. My stomach was one big knot, waiting for her to pull the damned trigger.

"I . . . don't know."

She coughed then and I said, "Let's get out of here so we can talk, Linda."

"No, no!"

"Linda—"

I'd never seen anyone with such vacant eyes before. I knew she was going to fire and that there was nothing I could do about it. I leaped for her anyway, just as an arm came through the doorway behind her and a hand took hold of her arm as she squeezed the trigger. Jack Dwyer pushed her arm up and her shot went into the ceiling. He reached around with his other hand and twisted the gun away from her.

"Jesus Christ," he said, "let's get out of here!"

7

Dwyer had indeed arrived late and, when he saw everyone outside and smelled the scent of a ripe one, he knew what was going on. He asked Vanguard about it, and George had told him that I'd gone downstairs to find the source of the smell. As it turned out, he was an ex-cop, too, as well as sometime actor and sometime P.I. It was just coincidence that he happened to land this role, so that he could be around to save my life. He'd told George to call the police, and came downstairs after me.

He told me all this at the Can-U-Drop-Inn over a beer, after the police had come and taken Linda Pollard away. Vanguard gave everyone the day off so that the theater could be cleared of the smell, and maybe even get the AC fixed.

"Why did she go down there?" Dwyer wondered aloud.

"I guess she was afraid I'd find the body."

"And it never occurred to her that that's what smelled?"

I shrugged and said, "I guess she'd never smelled a ripe one before, Jack. A lot of people haven't had that pleasure. Speaking of ripe ones, what'll happen to the show now?"

"I guess Vanguard will find himself two more virgins," Dwyer answered.

"And what about you?"

"I've about had it with this show. Vanguard's a prima donna, the leading man's gay, Onaly's number one virgin now, and she can't act worth a damn. I think I'll head back home."

"That means he'll have to replace you, too."

"That shouldn't be too hard. Mine wasn't much of a part, anyway." He swirled the beer at the bottom of his bottle and said, "They never are."

"Well," I said, "you've got my vote for performer of the year, the way you performed in that basement. I can't give you a Tony Award, but I can buy you another drink."

"Well," he said fatalistically, "I guess that's a start."

Double Edge

1

I have done laundry in Laundromats when being there was a bachelor's delight. In fact, up to about six months ago there were these three girls who were roommates living in the neighborhood, and they used to take turns doing the laundry. In the summer, those girls would come in dressed in shorts and halter-tops, and in the winter—when they took off their coats—they'd be wearing tight jeans and leg warmers. I mean, during that time I looked *forward* to doing the laundry. But they only lived there for a few months and then moved on, and the laundry went back to being a chore.

As a whole, the regular people who used this Laundromat—which was right on the corner of my block of Sackett Street in downtown Brooklyn—were pretty nice, but they were no great shakes to look at. Mrs. Goldstein was a woman in her late fifties who sort of adopted me—telling me what detergent to use, and what fabric softener, and "Oye, boychick, don't wash those in cold water!"—but she resembled the front end of a battleship; big "Mad Dog" Bolinsky, a bruiser who worked for the department of sanitation, looked like the *whole* battleship; Mr. Quinn, the Greek grocer, was in his late fifties also, and Mrs. Goldstein knew he was a widower just as he knew she was a widow.

And then there was Sam. Her real name was Samantha Karson, but she published her romance novels under the name "Kit Karson"—when she sold them, that is. Kit lived across the hall from me and once in a blue moon took time away from her typewriter to take in a movie with me, or to do her laundry. She wasn't the neatest person in the world, but she was pretty and easy to get along with.

When Linda Kellogg first walked into the Laundromat, nobody spoke to her beyond saying hello because that wasn't the way things were done. If she came back again, indicating that she might become a regular, then everyone would make an effort to get to know her. Mrs. Goldstein, of course, would make the initial approach, and then the introductions.

I noticed a few other things, though, that first day: Linda Kellogg wore a wedding ring, she had a bruise alongside her left eye, and as she was putting her clothes into the machine I saw a blouse with some blood on it. When she turned my way at one point I saw that her lip was split on the right side. This could all have been a result of anything from a mugging to a family dispute, and I really didn't give it a second thought after leaving the Laundromat.

The second time she came I found out her name—from Mrs. Goldstein, of course. During the course of the next few weeks she came every Friday—which was my regular day—and Mrs. Goldstein busied herself getting all the dope.

Linda usually had a small bruise here or there when she came—she *could* have been clumsy—but finally one Friday I noticed her talking to Mrs. Goldstein and crying. And that was when nice Mrs. Goldstein dragged her over to me.

"This quiet fella is Nick Delvecchio, Linda. He's a nice enough boy to be Jewish," Mrs. Goldstein said, which was the highest praise she could have given anyone. Then she added, "And he's the best private eye in Brooklyn," which was, at best, a dubious distinction.

"Hello," Linda said meekly.

"We've met in passing," I said.

"Linda has a problem, Nick," Mrs. Goldstein said, "and I told her you could help her."

"Is that a fact? What kind of problem?" I asked, looking at the mouse beneath her right eye.

I hated domestic cases.

"Tell him, dearie," Mrs. Goldstein urged Linda Kellogg.

Linda looked from Mrs. Goldstein to me a couple of times and I said, "Mrs. Goldstein, isn't your machine finished?"

"What?" The older woman looked behind her. Her wash was still being swirled about inside the machine. But never let it be said that Mrs. Goldstein couldn't take a hint.

"Hmm," she said, giving me the eye. "You help her, Nick. She's a nice girl."

"We'll see, Mrs. Goldstein."

"Hmm," she said again, and went back to her machine and her book.

"She's a nice old busybody," I told Linda.

"She's a nice woman."

"Do you want to tell me about it, or do you want to just make her think you're telling me?"

"I think I'll talk to you, Mr. Delvecchio. Even if you can't help me it might do me some good."

"All right," I said. "You don't mind if I fold my shirts while we talk, do you?"

"Oh," she said, as if the thought of a man folding his own belongings surprised her, "I'll do that."

She walked to my pile of laundry and began to talk and fold at the same time.

Put succinctly, it seemed that over the past few months—since they moved to this neighborhood—her husband had taken to beating her up on occasion. It always seemed to take place after he came home from work, even if she had cooked him his favorite dinner.

"Some nights he's fine, very loving," she said, "and other nights the slightest thing will set him off. I can't understand it."

"Do you know of any problems he might be having, either with family or his business?"

"No. He has no brothers or sisters, no aunts or uncles. Both his parents are dead."

"Do you think he might have a girlfriend?"

She looked at me with shock. "I *never* thought of that."

Was she on the level? Could she be that innocent?

"Linda, what is it you want me to do if not to find out about a girlfriend?"

"I—I want you to find out what is making him so angry. If he didn't come home angry, then he wouldn't have any reason to hit me."

"Have you thought about leaving him?"

"And go where? I have no family. I barely have any friends. I wouldn't have anyplace to go, Mr. Delvecchio. Besides, I love him. Will you help me?"

She finished folding my laundry and stared at me, waiting for my answer.

Helpless before the tragic look in her eyes I said, "I'll try."

"Thank you, Mr. Delvecchio, thank you."

I smiled halfheartedly and said, "Call me Nick."

2

Linda Kellogg's husband's name was Dan, and he worked as a dispatcher for a trucking firm with an office on Metropolitan Avenue in the Greenpoint section of Brooklyn. According to Linda, the position was a promotion for him, and the raise in salary was what enabled them to move to a better neighborhood. If they considered downtown Brooklyn a better neighborhood, I hated to think where they'd been living before.

I followed Dan Kellogg to and from work for a week and I found out nothing except that he didn't have a girlfriend which, for all I knew, might have been what was making him so angry. All he ever did was go home, sometimes stopping in a bar first, usually the same one. I followed him into the bar and watched him sit alone each time and drink a beer. One for the road before going home, I guessed.

I spoke to Linda after the week was up and she told me that Dan hadn't laid a finger on her since she hired me. I asked if she thought he knew about me and she said she was sure he didn't. She asked me to please stay on the case for a little while longer and I agreed.

After another week there was still no indication that *anything* was bothering Dan Kellogg, and still no sign of a girlfriend, either. So I figured the problem had resolved itself. I felt guilty taking a fee from Linda Kellogg, and when she asked me how much she owed me, I charged her for one week instead of two. We severed our business relationship in the same place it had started, the Laundromat.

After Linda left that day, Mrs. Goldstein came over. "Did you help her, Nicky?"

"I tried, Mrs. Goldstein, but I couldn't find out anything."

"You must have done something good, Nicky. The brute hasn't touched her in two weeks."

"I think the problem just solved itself."

Looking doubtful she said, "Mark my words, boychick. Problems very rarely solve themselves. Somebody usually has to solve them."

"I'll remember that," I said, and left with my clean laundry.

★ ★ ★ ★ ★

The following week I walked into the Laundromat and got the dirtiest look from Mrs. Goldstein she could muster.

"So, Mister Smart-Guy?" she asked, folding her arms across her ample chest.

"So what, Mrs. Goldstein?"

"What have you got to say for yourself?"

"About what?"

"Linda Kellogg."

"Mrs. Goldstein," I said, "could we stop playing twenty questions and just get down to the nitty-gritty?"

"Sure, tough-guy private eye talk you can do," she said, accusingly, "but when it comes to helping a little girl whose husband beats her up and puts her in the hospital—"

"Wait a minute," I said. "Are you telling me that Linda Kellogg is in the hospital?"

"That's what I said."

"What hospital?" I asked, putting my laundry basket down on her machine.

"That one near Atlantic Avenue."

"Long Island College Hospital?"

"That's the one."

"Mrs. Goldstein, will you do my laundry and hold it for me?"

"Are you going to the hospital?"

"Yes."

"Then I'll do your laundry, Mister Private Eye. You go and do what you should have done before, give that brute what-for."

I wasn't about to give her husband "what-for," but I did want to talk to Linda Kellogg. I wasn't feeling very good at that moment.

Linda was sharing a room with three other women. I

pulled the curtain all the way around her bed so that we could have some privacy. I was glad not to find her husband there.

"He's at work," she said. "He said he'll come up later."

"Tell me, what happened?"

She didn't look too bad, although her face was bruised and swollen so that she had to speak out of the corner of her mouth. Most of the damage had been done to the rib area, where he had broken two of them.

"I fell," she said.

"Linda, this is me you're talking to."

She looked directly at me and lied, and I had the feeling that she was trying to tell me something *by* lying to me.

"I fell," she said.

For some reason, she didn't want to admit—even to me— that her husband had hospitalized her.

"Who called for an ambulance?"

"Dan did."

"Did anyone call the police?"

"No police," she said, shaking her head.

"Linda, he could have killed you—"

"I want to hire you again," she said. "Find out what's making him so angry, Nick. Please!"

"I'll find out, all right," I said, "but I've already been paid and I didn't accomplish anything. This time it's on the house."

She closed her eyes and said, "Thank you."

When I left her she seemed to be asleep. I wondered what she had told the doctor about how she'd received her injuries.

I figured there was only one way I was going to find out what was making Dan Kellogg so violent. And that was to ask him.

3

Dan Kellogg's place of business was on Metropolitan Avenue, in an industrial area of Greenpoint, and I cabbed it there from the hospital.

Greenpoint is a funny section of Brooklyn, because in order to get there from some parts of the borough, you've got to go *into* Queens and then come *back* into Brooklyn. My driver, however, simply jumped onto the BQE—the Brooklyn-Queens Expressway—at the Atlantic Avenue entrance and jumped off at the McGuiness Boulevard exit, which left us just a few blocks from our destination.

When I got there I asked somebody where to find Dan Kellogg and was directed to the dispatcher's booth.

The man in the booth was a burly gent of about thirty, with thick brown hair and a mustache. It was the first time I had been closer to Dan Kellogg than fifty feet.

"Kellogg?" I said, leaning my head in the window.

"Just a sec," he said. He held a short conversation with someone over the radio, then turned to me and said, "Can I help you?"

"I'd like to talk to you if you can get relieved."

"Relieved?" he said, laughing. "Mister, you know how many trucks I'm juggling? I can't get just anybody to relieve me. What's it about?"

"It's about your wife."

"Linda?" he asked, frowning. "You from the hospital?"

"No," I said. "I'm investigating her 'accident.' "

His eyes widened momentarily, and then he licked his lips.

"There's a lounge down the hall," he said then. "Wait for me there, huh?"

"Sure."

There was another man in the lounge, but when I entered he left. It took Kellogg about five minutes to find somebody to relieve him.

"Why are the police interested in my wife's accident?" he asked, sitting next to me on a worn leather couch. "Did somebody say something . . . ?"

"About what, Mr. Kellogg?" I asked, prodding him.

"Nothing," he muttered. "What do you want to know?"

"I want to know how your wife received her injuries."

"Didn't the hospital tell you?"

"I want you to tell me."

"She fell . . . while changing a light bulb."

"Really?"

"Yes . . . really," he said. "That's what happened."

"Can I see your hands, Mr. Kellogg?"

"What for?"

"I'm curious."

"Look," Kellogg said, standing up and keeping his hands behind him, "I don't know what you're after, but I think I want to see your identification."

"That won't be necessary, Mr. Kellogg," I said, standing up. He was about my height, but he had me by twenty pounds. Still, I was pretty sure I could take him. Men who beat up on women can very rarely handle another man. "I'm not a policeman, and I never said I was."

His face turned red. He forgot about his hands and allowed them come into sight, and I could see that both hands had skinned knuckles. "Who the hell are you?"

"Somebody who'd like to know what kind of man takes

out his anger on a woman," I said. "And not just any woman, but his wife."

His hands closed into fists, but he held them at his side as he snapped, "Get out of here!"

"You beat up your wife, Mr. Kellogg," I said, taking out one of my business cards. "You know it, and I know it." I tucked the card into his shirt pocket and said, "I'm going to prove it, and I'm going to find out why, but for now just know this. If you touch that woman again, I'm personally going to break you in half."

4

I started tailing Kellogg again, but still to no avail. The day Linda got out of the hospital, he picked her up, brought her flowers, and took her home. They looked very cozy.

I went home that night and did something I hadn't done in a few days. I read the papers, going back three days. I was flipping through the news section when my eye was caught by a story on page three. It was about a truck hijacking, and the truck was one of the company's that Dan Kellogg worked for. The paper was dated the day he last abused his wife.

I picked up the phone and called Linda Kellogg, assuming—and hoping—that Dan Kellogg was at work. He was. I asked her if she could remember the last few dates that Dan had taken out his anger on her. She thought a few moments, checked a calendar, and gave me four dates that she thought were right.

"Tell me something else, Linda. You said the first beating took place after you moved here, right?"

"Yes."

"Did it also coincide with Dan's new job?"

"Well, of course. We moved here because he got the promotion."

"All right."

"Nick, have you found out something?"

"I don't know yet. I'll give you a call."

I hung up and left, heading for the main Brooklyn library near Grand Army Plaza. There I checked the files for the newspapers on the days after Dan Kellogg abused his wife. In each paper there was a report of a truck hijacking, and in two of the four cases, the trucks were from Dan Kellogg's company.

And he was the new dispatcher. How difficult would it be for him to give somebody information, on what a particular truck was carrying, and then to set up a hijacking?

I made photocopies of the stories and left the library. It was dark, and I started walking so I could think. There was one thing that bothered me. Of the five hijackings I had read about, only three involved trucks that belonged to Kellogg's firm. If Kellogg was involved, then what about the other two? And why, after each hijacking, did he go home angry enough to beat his wife? Could he have been involved against his will? Was *that* what was making him so angry?

When I got home I called Linda again and asked her if her husband was home from work yet. He wasn't.

"Did you find out—"

"I have to find him first, Linda, and then I can answer your question. I'll call."

I had followed Kellogg enough times after work to know where he might be.

On more than one occasion he had dropped into the same bar on the way home, a place on Fourth Avenue. I took a cab over there and went inside looking for him. He was seated at the bar, with a mug of beer in front of him. I slid onto the stool next to him and said, "Hi, Danny, boy."

"What are you doing here?"

"I came to talk to you."

"Well, I don't want to talk to you."

"I think you'd better."

He turned his head and looked at me. I had never seen such empty eyes before.

"Look, friend, I know you're trying to help Linda, but you don't know—"

"I know more than you think."

"Like what?"

"Like about the hijackings."

Surprise brought him off his stool. "You think you know about that, huh?" he demanded. "Big shot P.I., huh?" He faced me, clenching his hands angrily.

"You want to try me, Kellogg?"

"Yeah," he said, and hit me.

The blow didn't hurt that much, but it sure as hell surprised me. And it knocked me off my stool and onto the floor.

"Come on," Kellogg said, standing over me, "get up. Let's see how tough you are."

"Take it easy," I said. I was seeing the Dan Kellogg that his wife saw. "What the hell is making you so mad?"

"I thought you knew."

Yeah, I thought I knew, too. But I'd also had him pegged as a wife beater who'd back away from a real fight. I could be wrong as often as I was right.

I got to my feet and said, "Wait a second—" but he swung again. I stepped away from it. "Kellogg—" I said, but he wasn't listening. The emptiness that had been in his eyes had been replaced by rage. He advanced on me and swung a third time.

I stepped *inside* this blow and landed one of my own to his belly. He was softer than he looked there, and all of the air—

and fight—went out of him. He fell to the floor on his butt, gasping for air.

I glanced around the bar. What few people were there decided that the fight was over and looked away.

"You want a beer?" the bartender asked me.

"Why not?"

By the time he brought my beer Kellogg had his breath back.

"I'm gonna help you up," I said. "If you swing at me again we're gonna go all the way. Got it?"

"Yeah," he said hoarsely.

I helped him up and onto his stool again, then took the one next to him.

"What do you know about these hijackings?" he asked.

"It wasn't hard to figure. The last five times you hit Linda were days following a hijacking, and the hijackings started after you got promoted to dispatcher."

"Yeah," he said. "It's easy for me to let them know which trucks to hit, where and when."

"Two of the trucks weren't yours, though."

"That's no problem. I talk to dispatchers from other firms. I can get information."

"Why are you doing it?"

He didn't answer that right away. He said, "Look, I admit that I've . . . hit Linda a couple of times, but this last time, when she went to the hospital . . . it wasn't me. I swear it wasn't."

"Sure. She fell screwing in a light bulb."

"No . . . it was Harry."

"Who's Harry?"

"Her cousin, Harry Sullivan."

"Her own cousin beat her up?"

"That's right."

"Why?"

"It was a message to me."

"Wait," I said. "Are you telling me that this cousin Harry is involved in the hijackings?"

"You're getting it now," he said. "When he found out from Linda that I'd been promoted, he came to see me. He's got a record, see, and he saw my promotion as a chance for him and his friends to make some money."

"And they got you to go along by threatening Linda?"

"That, and he said he'd tell my boss I was passing information, just to get me fired."

"Nice family."

"He's a bum," he said, and I was tempted to tell him that he was, too. This Harry threatens to hurt Linda, so Kellogg goes along with the hijackings—and then *he* hurts Linda.

"Did you tell Linda?"

"No, but after this last hijacking I tried to pull out, and Harry went to see her."

"So now she knows?"

"Yes."

"Why didn't she say something?"

"Hey, he's her family."

One thing I had to say for Linda Kellogg, she was loyal to the men in her family, even if it was misplaced loyalty. Still, she had come to me—looking for somebody to make things right.

"And you let this bum get away with knocking your wife around?"

"Yeah," he said, wrapping his hand around his beer mug, "yeah, I did . . . but no more."

"You ready to turn them in?"

"How? I'd have to turn myself in."

"We'll talk to the police together. I know a lieutenant named Wager who would be very interested in hearing your story."

"And then what?"

"And then they'll set something up with you, to catch the hijackers in the act."

"Will I go to jail?"

"I doubt it. You were coerced, and you'll cooperate. I don't think you'll go to jail." I leaned closer to him and said, "*I'll* see that you go to jail, though, if you ever lay a hand on Linda again."

He said he wouldn't and for Linda's sake I hoped he was telling the truth. In his anger and frustration he had lashed out at the easiest prey available, but deep down there was another anger, this one directed at his wife. It was *her* cousin who was forcing him to do these things, so it had to be *her* fault.

His was a double-edged anger, carved out of frustration and guilt. I could help with some of it, but the rest was up to him. He still had to come to terms with the fact that he was a man who battered his wife because of something *he* couldn't handle.

Turnabout

1

Frank Cabretta looked every bit as dangerous in jail as he had looked out. The fact that he was wearing prison clothes diminished his stature not one iota. He sat in his plastic chair as if he were sitting in the leather chair behind his huge oak desk in his luxurious home in Long Island.

"Nick," he said.

"I thought I told you a long time ago not to call me that."

Cabretta smiled contemptuously.

"What are you going to do," he asked, "send me to prison?"

I gave way to a small smile and said, "You have a point."

Even here Cabretta was entitled to certain privileges, such as a private meeting room on demand that was usually reserved for lawyer/client relationships. I was a private detective, not a lawyer, and Cabretta was certainly not a client. On the contrary, five years ago I was a cop, and Cabretta was behind bars with my compliments.

That made Cabretta's "summons" even more curious.

"Have a seat," Cabretta said. "I have something I want to talk to you about."

"What makes you think I'm interested in anything you'd have to say to me?"

Cabretta, a good-looking man in his late forties, smiled and said, "The fact that you're here answers that question."

"I'm here because I was paid five hundred dollars to come."

"Five?" Cabretta said, showing mild surprise. "I told my lawyer to offer you two."

"He did," I said, and left it at that.

"I see," Cabretta said. "Will you have that seat?"

I hesitated, then said, "Why not?" and sat across the table from the ex-drug king turned prisoner.

Cabretta turned to the guard who was standing inside the door and said, "Get lost."

"I can't—"

"Beat it, screw!"

The guard looked at me and I said, "It's all right."

"I'll be right outside."

"Stay away from the door!" Cabretta called after the guard as he left. "Fuckin' walls have the biggest ears you ever saw in here," he said. "All right, then, let's get to it. I want to hire you."

"That's a laugh."

"Nevertheless," Cabretta said, "it's true."

Warily, I asked, "To do what?"

"Since I've been here my wife has either visited me or written to me at least once a week, sometimes one of each a week."

"So? She's a faithful wife."

Cabretta frowned and said, "That's what I want you to find out."

"Why?"

"I haven't seen her or heard from her in a month."

"Maybe she's sick."

"I don't think so. I think there's something else going on, and I want you to find out what."

"Why not have one of your goons outside do the job?" I asked.

"Because I want it done on the qt," Cabretta said, "and I don't trust anyone else to do it but you."

"Why's that?"

"You put me here," Cabretta said, "that means you're good at what you do. I want to hire the best."

"I'm good, but I'm not the best."

"I'll take my chances with you, Nick."

"I told you—"

Cabretta raised his hand to stay the objection and said, "Sorry . . . *Mister* Delvecchio."

"Let me get this straight," I said. "You want me to find out why your wife hasn't written or come to see you in a month."

"That's right."

"And then what?"

"And then come back here and tell me."

"You don't want me to report to your attorney?"

"He doesn't know why I'm seeing you today."

"You haven't told your attorney?" I asked, in surprise.

"I told you," Cabretta said, "I don't trust anyone on this but you."

I studied Cabretta for a few long moments. His dark hair had begun to show some gray while he'd been inside, but he looked as if he were still keeping himself in shape. He looked fit, with the build of a man ten years his junior.

"Why should I do this for you?"

"I knew you'd ask me that," Cabretta said. "You owe me."

I snorted and said, "For what?"

"For putting me here," Cabretta said, showing the first signs of agitation. "For taking away five years of my life, that's why!"

"You deserve to be in here, Cabretta," I replied casually. "You *belong* in here, and for a lot longer than five years."

Cabretta stiffened his jaw and for a moment I thought he was going to explode. I watched as the man brought his fabled temper under control, and thought that at least he had learned something during his stay here.

"All right," Cabretta finally said, "name your fee, then. You work for people for money, right? Well, I've got money. Name your price."

My regular price was two hundred and fifty dollars a day plus expenses. Things had been rough during the past year and at times the price had come down as low as one hundred and fifty.

"Three hundred and fifty a day, plus expenses."

Cabretta never blinked.

"Take the case and I'll have my attorney pay you a week's retainer."

"And if I don't catch her doing anything . . . wrong during that time?"

"Come and tell me, and then we're quits."

"And if I find that she is seeing someone?"

"Same thing."

I studied him for a minute and then said, "And then she ends up, dead, right? Thanks, but no thanks, Frankie. I don't want that on my conscience."

Cabretta looked appalled and said, "My own wife? And even if she wasn't my wife, I don't do business that way. You know that, Ni—Delvecchio."

He was right. I did know that—but this didn't sound like business, and she *was* his wife. I was sure that all he wanted was confirmation that his wife was cheating on him, and then he'd have her taken care of. I also knew that if I didn't take the job, someone else would.

"All right, Frank," I said, finally.

"You'll work for me?"

"Sure," I said, with a shrug. "Your money's as good as anyone else's, right?"

"It's better than anyone else's . . . Nick." He spoke my name with a smug look on his face. "Can I call you Nick, now that you work for me?"

I grinned at him and said, "No."

I left the prison, knowing that I had made a decision and I had to stick to it. I didn't like it, but I knew I'd stick to it.

2

The call from Frankie Cabretta's attorney had come in early that morning. I had just stepped out of the shower and was dripping on the cheap linoleum as I picked up the receiver.

"Delvecchio," I said, holding the receiver with my right hand and drying my hair with my left. The air-conditioning from the window unit felt cold on my wet, naked flesh.

"Nick Delvecchio, please," a man's voice said. It sounded vaguely familiar, but I couldn't place it.

"This is he."

"Oh, I was expecting, er, a secretary."

"My secretary's gone out to pick up some more Sweet 'n Low," I said. "We ran out. Who's calling me, please?"

"Mr. Delvecchio, my name is Walter Koenig. Do you remember me?"

"Koenig," I said, repeating the name once. It was all I need to remember the man. I stopped drying my hair and dropped my hand to my side, still holding the towel.

"Sure, Mr. Koenig, I remember you. You're Frankie Cabretta's attorney—or at least, you were five years ago." I didn't bother disguising the dislike in my tone, for both men, lawyer and client.

"I still am, Mr. Delvecchio, and that is why I am calling you," Koenig said. "Would you be able to come to my office this afternoon?"

"What for?"

"To discuss the possibility of, er, employment."

"By you? Don't you have staff investigators, counselor, or have you fallen on hard times?" I asked. I almost said, "Have you fallen on hard times, *too*," but stopped myself in time.

"Uh, I would prefer not to discuss this over the phone, Mr. Delvecchio. If you would come to my office, it would be, ah, more convenient."

"For who?"

"For, uh, me, of course," the man said. "It would also be to your benefit, however."

"How's that?"

"I would pay you two hundred dollars."

I tried to keep my tone neutral, even though my heart had leaped into my throat.

"Just to come to your office and listen."

"That's right."

"The money would be nonrefundable?"

"Of course."

I paused a moment, then decided, what the hell, what the hell!

"My fee is two hundred and *fifty* dollars a day."

There was no hesitation on Walter Koenig's part whatsoever. "Done."

The clock on my wall said it was 9:00 A.M.

"I'll be there by eleven, Mr. Koenig."

"Ten would be preferable, Mr. Delvecchio."

"Eleven, counselor."

"Ah, yes, of course," Koenig said. "I will look forward to seeing you at eleven."

I hung up the phone and kept my hand on it. I hadn't seen a day's pay in over a month. So what if I had to suffer the company of slime like Walter Koenig for a few minutes. I'd listen to what he had to say, turn him down flat, and walk out two hundred and fifty dollars richer, without the slightest hint of guilt.

3

Koenig's office was in a building on Court Street, a healthy hike from my apartment on Sackett Street. I remember now wondering five years ago why Frank Cabretta's attorney didn't have an office on Park Avenue, across the Brooklyn Bridge in Manhattan?

The front door had gold lettering on the cherry oak wood that said WALTER KOENIG, ATTORNEY, and I entered without bothering to knock.

The woman behind the desk in the reception room looked up and gave me a professional smile—the kind that fully occupied the mouth and teeth and never invaded the eyes—and said, "May I help you, sir?"

She was in her early forties, but she was handsomely made up to hide the lines I knew had to be there. Still, she went right along with the rest of the room, which gave off the impression of class.

"I have an appointment with Mr. Koenig."

"Mr. Delvecchio?"

"That's right."

"You may go right in. He's expecting you."

When she said "He," I knew that she automatically capitalized the word.

"Thank you," I said, but the receptionist had already

turned her attention back to her computer terminal.

I went to the unmarked door the receptionist had indicated and opened it, again without knocking.

Koenig was behind a cluttered desk that surprised me. For one thing it was rather small, and that and the fact that it *was* cluttered did not go along with the impression presented by the reception area, and the receptionist. This room—small, sensibly furnished, and anything but neat—seemed to reflect more of the man than the reception room did—which was, of course, only natural. After all, he spent most of his time in here.

I might have liked him for that if I hadn't known he was Cabretta's lawyer.

"Ah, Mr. Delvecchio," Walter Koenig said, rising. "I'm so glad you came."

"I'm not sure I am," I said honestly.

"Perhaps, if I were to write you a check—"

Not wishing to seem *that* mercenary, I said, "You can do that later. Why don't you tell me why I'm here?"

"Please, take a seat."

There was only one to take, a straight-backed wooden chair in front of his desk, and I took it.

Koenig was in his mid-forties, a tall, slender but well-built man with curly brown hair the color of shoe polish. I couldn't help but wonder if he dyed it.

"My client wishes to engage your services."

"By client you mean Frank Cabretta?"

"Yes."

I started to stand and said, "We have nothing further to talk about."

"Oddly enough," he said, "you are correct."

"What?" I asked, stopping midway out of the chair, my knees still bent.

"You see," he said sheepishly, "I know that Mr. Cabretta wishes to hire you, but I haven't the faintest idea why."

"He hasn't told you?" I asked. "His lawyer?"

"Ah, no, he hasn't."

"Isn't that rather odd?"

"I thought so," he said. "I also told him—as you mentioned on the phone—that I have my own investigators. He was quite adamant that he wanted you."

"Why?"

"Alas, I can't answer that," he said. "I've been instructed to pay you for consulting with me, and to ask you to go and see him."

"In prison?"

"Yes."

I sat back down because I was feeling silly—and my legs were getting tired.

"I don't understand."

"To be frank, I don't, either. I'm rather anxious for you to see him so that I can also find out what is going on."

"I put him away," I said. "At least, my testimony did. It's ludicrous that I'd go up and see him."

Koenig smiled and said, "A fascinating prospect, isn't it?"

Against my better judgment I admitted to myself that he was right. It was fascinating, and I knew that my curiosity would not allow me to pass this up.

"All right," I said. "I'll go."

"I'll write your check for the consultation," he said.

"Double it."

"What?"

"Two hundred and fifty for coming here, and another two hundred and fifty for the trip to Ossining."

"I don't think—"

"You want me to go to Sing Sing, counselor, you've got to

pay my way." I shrugged, as if to say, that's the way it is, take it or leave it.

He took it.

He pulled a checkbook from his desk drawer, wrote me a check, and handed it across the desk to me. I took it, looked at it, tucked it into my wallet, and stood up.

"I suppose you'll clear the way for this," I said.

"I'll make some calls, yes."

I stared at him and then said, "You've already made them, haven't you?"

He smiled and said, "How did you guess?"

"I didn't guess," I said, "I know, just by looking at you."

"You're a very good detective."

"You're damned right I am," I said, and then added before leaving: "Just ask your client."

I wasn't a detective when I put Cabretta away, just a patrolman who happened to be in the right place at the right time, but I wasn't about to let that ruin a good exit line.

4

When I got back to Brooklyn, I went right to Koenig's office again and presented myself to his secretary.

"I'm afraid I don't have an appointment this time," I told her.

"Yes, you do," she said. "Go right in."

I went into Koenig's office and sat in his visitor's chair. There was a brown, ten-by-thirteen manila envelope on my side of his desk.

"Everything you need to know about Carla Cabretta is in there," he said. "Where she has her hair done, where she has her car serviced, where her health club is—"

"The only thing we don't know," I said, sliding her photo out of the envelope, "is who's fucking her."

"If she is having an affair," Koenig said stiffly, "that is up to you to find out."

I studied the color photo. It looked like a studio print. Just a head shot—but what a head! If the colors were to be believed her hair was chestnut, her eyes green. She was a beautiful woman. There was a second picture, as well. This was a candid shot of her leaving someplace, wearing a leotard. It must have been taken in front of her health club. She was tall, with long, long legs, a tiny waist, and small, high, firm breasts and wide shoulders. No body builder, Carla Cabretta, but extremely fit.

"Classy looking," I said.

"Yes, she is."

"All right, Walter," I said, using his first name to his dismay. "I'll get right on it."

"Yes," he said, "you do that." He couldn't wait for me to leave. Now that I was working for Frank Cabretta he couldn't waste his time on me. To him, I was just another employee.

That was okay with me. I didn't like him all that much, either.

"You'll notice on the back of the color photo there are two addresses," Koenig said. "One is the house in Long Island, and one is an apartment she has taken in Park Slope."

"Does Frank know about the apartment?"

"Of course," Koenig said. "If I know about it, Frank knows."

"Of course," I said, standing, "how silly of me. If he ever found out that you were keeping anything from him—"

"I wouldn't," Koenig said, "and if I were you, I wouldn't think about it, either."

"I assume I'll be reporting to you?"

"That is correct."

"Well, I'd better get to it, then."

"I would appreciate a report at the end of each day."

"By telephone all right?"

"Fine."

"Fine," I said, and he narrowed his eyes as if he suspected I was mimicking him.

And, of course, I was.

5

Carla Cabretta's Brooklyn apartment was in the yuppified Park Slope section of Brooklyn. Her health club was also in that area, which meant that I didn't have to go very far from my own neighborhood to tail her. If and when I needed a car, I had access to a friend's mint-condition '76 Grand Prix.

I was right behind her for three straight days, and although she had met two different men for lunch, she had neither gone home with anyone, nor brought anyone home with her. I was starting to get the feeling that maybe Carla wasn't really cheating on Frank, she just wanted to get away from being Mrs. Cabretta.

I called Koenig at the end of each of the first five days. On the evening of the sixth day I got to achieve one of those goals.

She'd had dinner with two lady friends, probably women she had met at the health club, from the way they looked. They were all very fit, and taut, and as a group they skillfully fended off all advances. They separated outside the restaurant, a tiny, hole-in-the-wall bistro on Atlantic Avenue, and Carla drove right home in her little blue Mercedes.

She had an apartment on the second floor of a converted

brownstone, and I watched her fit her key into the front door. I always waited until she was inside before breaking off the surveillance. I watched until her light went on in front of the building and then started my motor, getting ready to leave. I took one last look at the front of the building, and abruptly shut the motor.

There was a shadow on the stairs, someone at the door, fiddling with it. It wasn't a resident, because by now I knew most of them. As I watched the door opened, illuminating for one moment a man clad in dark clothes as he entered and closed the door behind him.

It could have been anything, of course. Might even have been a simple burglar, but I didn't want to take the chance. I got out of the Grand Prix, first taking a .38 from the glove compartment, and crossed the street. I don't carry a gun as a matter of course, but all along I had the feeling I was going to need one. The .38 was my off-duty gun when I was a cop.

It was after ten and dark, and the street was empty. I already knew that there were very few kids on this block, and for the most part they rolled up the streets early.

When I reached the front door, I couldn't really see the lock well enough to tell how he had opened it. I took out my trusty lock picks and fitted them both into the lock. Unlike television and the movies, you need two hands and two instruments to properly pick a lock.

It took me a minute but I finally opened the door and slipped inside. I put the lock picks in my left pocket and took the gun out of my right.

I went through the second door and stood still a moment. I thought I could hear floorboards creaking, but that could have been from any apartment. I went to the stairs and started up. Carla's apartment was on the second floor, but the stairs were split into two flights, with a landing in between. There was supposed to be a light over the first landing, but someone had apparently unscrewed the light bulb. Either that, or it had conveniently gone out. I was on the landing when I heard her scream. My first instinct was to run up the second flight, but I held myself back. Sure enough, a shadow appeared below me, at the foot of the steps.

"Stop right there!" I said.

"Shit!" he said, and I was already on my belly when I saw the muzzle flash from his gun. His bullet went over my head. I fired and heard him cry out as the bullet struck him.

Now I ran up to the second floor and stopped when I saw her door was open a crack. I backed up two steps and leaned over so I could watch the door. Finally, the second man became impatient, and the door opened wider.

"Gino?" a voice called. "Gino, did you get him?"

"Uh," I said.

"Gino?"

"I got 'im," I said.

"Gino . . . that ain't you!"

The door started to close and I thought I'd blown it. Suddenly, though, the man staggered out into the hall, as if pushed from behind. Before he could regain his balance I was in the hall, pointing my gun.

"Don't be stupid," I called out, but obviously I was years too late. Off balance, he still squeezed the trigger of his gun. The bullet struck the wall next to me, and I fired twice, because I was taking no chances. Both bullets hit home, and he slid down the wall, leaving a bloody trail on it that tenants could either clean or talk about for years to come.

I ran down the hall, took a moment to check him, then went into the apartment. Carla Cabretta was on the floor near the door, bound hand and foot and gagged. Obviously, she had managed to hop over to the door and shove the man out into the hall.

I untied her, but kept my gun in my hand. I hadn't had time to check and make sure the first man was dead.

"Thanks for pushing him," I said.

"Thanks for being here," she said, rubbing her wrists.

I helped her to her feet, then closed and locked the apartment door.

"By the way," she said calmly, "who are you and how come you *are* here?"

She didn't strike me as the type to scream. She told me later that the man had twisted her arm so that she yelled out in pain, I suppose for my benefit. Her scream was supposed to make me rush up the steps, unaware that there was a man behind me who intended to kill me.

"Before we go into that," I said, "let's get our story straight, or we'll both be spending most of the night in a police station."

I looked at her for a moment. This was the first time I had seen her this close up. Her photos had not done her justice. Neither had watching her from across the street.

"Now that you've inspected the merchandise," she said wryly, "would you tell me what you're talking about?"

"That many shots will not go unnoticed," I said. "The police will be here soon. We've got to agree on an explanation for all of this."

"Why?" she said. "Why should I tell them anything but the truth? That I don't know any of the three of you?"

"Because I just killed two men to save our lives."

"Our lives?"

"Yes."

She frowned at me and asked, "You don't work for my husband, do you?"

I hesitated, then said, "Yes and no."

"I can't wait to hear the explanation for that one."

6

When the cops arrived, we had our story straight. Mrs. Cabretta told them who she was, and that she had hired me to be her bodyguard because she'd been getting some threatening phone calls. I showed them my P.I. ticket, my gun permit, and dropped some names from their precinct, the seven-seven. When the detectives arrived, I knew one of them. His name was Weinstock, and he usually partnered with Vito Matucci. At one time Matucci and I were patrol-car partners.

"Where's Vito, Weinstock?" I asked.

"You know this guy?" one of the uniformed cops asked.

"Yes, I know him," Weinstock said.

"Good," the cop said, handing Weinstock my ticket and my permit, "he's all yours."

The uniforms left, and the two bodies had been removed from the halls. All that was left behind was some blood.

"This is Simmons," Weinstock said, indicating his partner. "Matucci's got the flu." Simmons was impressive. He was the biggest black man I'd ever seen, with shoulders like the wingspan of a 747. We nodded at each other.

I didn't miss Matucci. His absence meant I didn't have to match insults with anyone.

"Tell it to me," Weinstock said.

I gave him the same story I had given the uniforms, and then Carla backed me up. Weinstock handed me back my goods.

"Come into the station in the morning, Delvecchio, and make a statement."

"Sure."

"And bring the lady."

Carla smiled at him from the sofa.

"You better save that one, Weinstock," I said. "I don't think you'll ever get one like it."

Weinstock looked at Carla, then said, "I think you're right."

He tapped Simmons on the arm and led the way out the door.

I looked at Carla and said, "You were great. Thanks."

"Delvecchio," she said, as if tasting my name. "Aren't you the policeman whose testimony sent my husband to prison?"

"I was, yes."

"Now that that's over with," she said, "you want to tell me what's going on?"

I sat next to her on the sofa. My nostrils filled up with her perfume. It was a very nice scent. Up close like this I could see that she was about thirty-five, a good ten or twelve years younger than her husband.

"Mrs. Cabretta—"

"Please," she said, "don't call me that. After saving my life you're at least entitled to call me Carla."

"At least," I said.

We stared at each other in silence for a few moments, and then I said, "Carla, your husband hired me to follow you, and find out why you haven't come to see him during the past month."

"Why would he do that?" she asked, frowning. "He knows why I haven't come to see him. I want a divorce."

"You told him that?"

"The last time I saw him. I told him I wouldn't be back to see him, either."

"Do you have a lawyer?"

"No," she said, "Frank said that Walter would take care of everything."

"Frank agreed to the divorce?"

She shrugged and said, "He loves me, and wants me to be happy. So tell me, Mr. Delvecchio, why would he send you to follow me to find out something he already knows?"

"I think it's fairly obvious, Carla."

She thought it over a moment, and then said, "You mean he sent those two men to kill me?"

"No," I said, "he sent one to kill you, and one to kill me."

Now she was getting it.

"He was going to have me killed, and frame you for it?"

"He was probably going to make it look like we killed each other."

"That son of a bitch!"

"Good," I said. "I thought I was going to have to convince you."

"You don't have to convince me," she said, "but I'd like you to tell me what we can do about it. Killing two of his men isn't going to stop him."

"I'm sure they weren't his men," I said. "I'm sure Koenig hired these two guys free-lance."

"There is plenty of free-lance talent around," she said. She wasn't only beautiful, she was sharp. I liked her. She knew what was going on.

"I have a plan."

She smiled and said, "I hoped you would."

"Why don't you make us some coffee and I'll tell you about it."

7

We presented ourselves at the offices of Walter Koenig, Esq. at 10:00 A.M. the next morning—after a stop over at the seven-seven precinct.

After I had outlined my plan to her the night before she had smiled and said, "That's mean. Oh, that's delicious."

The word "delicious" sounded entirely natural coming out of her mouth.

"You don't have an appointment, this time," the secretary said as we entered.

"That's all right," I said, "just tell him I'm here, and then we won't need you. We can get our own coffee."

"I don't get cof—just a minute," she said, annoyed. "I'll announce you."

"Why don't you go out and get a donut or something, honey?" I picked up her purse and handed it to her. "We'll announce ourselves."

She looked at us, then took her bag and walked out the door.

"I'll wait here until you call me," Carla said.

I nodded and walked into Walter Koenig's office.

"What are you doing here?" he demanded. "Where's my secretary?" If he was surprised to see me alive, he hid it well.

"She said something about going out to get a donut."

He stood up and said, "I have a court date, Mr. Delvecchio. What do you want?"

"I want the rest of my fee," I said. 'The job is done."

"What?"

"I know who's been porking Mrs. Cabretta."

"You know—" He stopped and frowned. "Who?"

I smiled at him and said, "You."

He looked stunned.

"That's ridiculous. I've never laid a hand on Carla. What are you trying to pull?"

"What do you think Frankie will say when I give him my report, Walter?"

"You wouldn't—he would never believe you."

"I have a witness."

"A . . . witness? How could you have a witness? I've never touched her, I tell you. I swear!"

Only someone who was telling the truth could be that indignant, but it didn't matter that he was telling the truth.

"An unimpeachable witness."

"That's not possible," he said. "Who could the witness be?"

I smiled, walked to the door, and opened it. Carla Cabretta walked in and smiled at Koenig. I left the door ajar.

"I'm sorry, darling," she said, "but he beat it out of me."

He gaped at her, then at me, and then understanding dawned in his eyes.

"You're framing me."

"Why not?" I asked. "You were ready not only to frame me for killing Mrs. Cabretta, but to kill me as well."

"You were never to be killed," Koenig said, "just framed."

"Well, that makes all the difference in the world, Walter," I said. "Turnabout is fair play. How do you like the frame?"

"I don't," he said. "If you tell Frank . . . he'll have me killed."

He looked at Carla for support and she said, "I'll shed lover's tears at your funeral, darling."

"You can't—" he said to her, and then he looked at me and said, "You can't—"

"Don't worry, Walter," I said, "I'm a reasonable man. We can work something out."

He stared at us for a few moments, and then sighed and said, "What do you want me to do?"

"I'd like you to meet a friend of mine," I said. I went to the door and opened it all the way. Detective Weinstock walked in. After we stopped at the precinct to make our statements I had convinced him to come with us to Koenig's office.

"The detective will be happy to take your statement," I said to Koenig.

I took Carla's arm and led her out of the office.

Down on the street I said to Carla, "I don't think you'll have any trouble getting that divorce now. In fact, with the extra time this murder conspiracy will add to your husband's sentence, you might even be able to get the Catholic Church to grant you an annulment."

Carla Cabretta said, "I'm very impressed, Nick . . . and grateful. Perhaps you'll let me express my gratitude, over dinner?"

"You gonna chase me home, like you did last night?"

Her delicious mouth smiled and she said, "Why don't you take a chance and find out?"

Laying Down to Die

1

All death is tragic. Particularly when it's accidental. After all, someone dying as the result of a fluke, or an act of carelessness? Tragic, to say the least. Now natural causes, that's probably the least tragic of all. I mean, what can you possibly do about that? A man goes to the doctor one week and is given a clean bill of health, and the very next week he clutches his head and drops to the floor, dead. Happens every day, right?

So where does murder fit into this equation? Well, in my opinion, murder is just a step below accident. What keeps murder from being at the top of the list is that it is a deliberate act. One person sets out to take the life of another person. There's nothing "tragic" about that—it's just a damned shame!

And where does suicide fit in?

Who the hell knows?

I stared at the casket from my seat in the back of the chapel. I chose to sit there alone because I was not a family member. In fact, I was not even a close friend. I was someone who had known the deceased in high school, and met her again eighteen years later for one evening—and then she was dead.

High school was not the favorite time of my life. I know people of varying ages who claim that, given the chance, they'd go back in time to their high school days. In my opinion, people like that just can't deal with being grown up. Given the opportunity to go back to the happiest time of my life, I'd stay right where I am. I guess that means I haven't had the happiest time of my life yet. So what? I think that's good. Gives me something to look forward to—and to me, looking forward is miles better than looking back.

Last week, however, I *did* step back in time, sort of. It was the evening of my eighteenth high school reunion. I had been invited to reunions before—the tenth, and the fifteenth—and had not gone. Why I decided to go to this one is still a mystery to me. (Why they even had an eighteenth reunion is a mystery to me. Don't they usually have them at ten, fifteen, and twenty, like that?) Well, it wasn't a *total* mystery to me why I was there. Sam had something to do with it.

Samantha Karson is my neighbor. She lives in the apartment across from me. We're friends—*just* friends, although why that situation hasn't . . . progressed after living across from each other for a few years *is* a mystery. Sam's a beautiful blonde with the body of Bardot, the hair and eyelashes of Sissy Spacek, and a face that's all her own.

The day that I received the invitation to the reunion was an afternoon that we had decided to have lunch together at a nearby diner.

"That's when you graduated?" she asked, looking at the invitation.

"You *know* how old I am, Sam."

"I know." Her smile was teasing. "It just looks so . . . archaic in print."

She put the invitation down and looked at me across her turkey club. Sam was on another diet. She was a full-bodied young woman who, as far as I could see, was proud of that fact. Why then was she constantly trying to lose five pounds?

"I think you should go."

"Why?"

"Why shouldn't you go. Didn't you have some friends in high school?"

"Sure, I had *some* . . ."

"But not a lot?"

"A few."

"Any girlfriends?"

"A few."

"Aren't you curious about what's happened to them? What kind of adults they've become?"

"No."

"Why not?"

"I might be disappointed."

She stared at me then. "Or maybe you think they'll be disappointed in you?"

Okay, so I decided to go to the damned thing . . .

The reunion was held in Marine Park, at a hall on Avenue N called the Something-or-other Château. I admit to some degree of nervousness as I entered through the front door. That disappeared, however, when I saw this huge apparition from the past advancing on me. He had his arms spread wide, a wingspread I readily recognized as belonging to Tony "Mitts" Bologna.

"Nicky-D, you sonofabitch!" he shouted, and crushed me in a bear hug that took me to within an inch of my life. As it was, I didn't think I'd ever be able to have kids.

"Tony Mitts!" I surprised myself because I was shouting back at him with almost as much enthusiasm.

It was then that I silently thanked Sam for talking me into going.

It was much later when I cursed her for it . . .

★ ★ ★ ★ ★

From my vantage point in the back of the chapel I could see Tony Bologna's back. His shoulders were shaking. Sitting to his right was his mother. Her shoulders were ramrod straight. On his left was the mother of the deceased. She was alternately patting and rubbing his back, the way I thought his own mother should have been doing.

I looked up toward the casket again, where Mary Ann Grosso was lying, all dressed and made up to look "good" in death. God, I hated when people said of the dead, "They look *good!*"

Mary Ann Grosso simply looked dead, which was a far cry from the way she had looked the night of the reunion . . .

Tony Mitts was just the start of it at the reunion. In rapid order I met up with Sammy Carter, Joey "the Nose" Bagaletti, and Vito "the Ace" Pricci. The four of us used to hang out together in high school, which a lot of people found odd, because while three of us were Italian, Sammy was black. We were fond of telling people he was "Black" Italian. Among ourselves, we also said that if anybody didn't like it, "Fuck 'em."

We staked out a place at the bar, watching the girls go by.

"Boy," Vito said, "most of these girls have really porked up, huh?"

"Especially the Italian ones," Sammy said, nodding his head in agreement.

"What are you complainin' about?" Tony said to Sammy. "I thought skinny black guys like you liked your women big and fat."

Sammy fixed Tony with a hard stare. "You gonna start that 'fat-assed black girl' stuff again, Tony Mitts? You were always doin' that in high school and I didn't like it then!"

"Yeah, yeah . . ." Tony said.

Eighteen years ago Tony was always teasing Sammy about his girlfriends having big asses. It was true, but Sammy had always acted like he didn't like it.

I examined my three high school friends critically. Tony had always been big, well over six feet, but he'd never been fat, and he still wasn't. He'd kept himself in remarkable shape, but then as an athlete he would. We called him Tony "Mitts" because he had hands the size of catcher's mitts. It was better, he said, than what they used to call him in grammar school—Tony "Baloney." Ah, grammar school kids had no imagination.

Sammy was as skinny as ever, and his hair had receded to the halfway point on his head. The bald part of his head, though, gleamed, the way Lou Gossett's and George Foreman's heads do. I wondered why he didn't just shave it.

Vito had gone to fat, which he was always threatening to do in high school. His arms, though, still threatened to burst the seams of his clothes. We would have nicknamed him "the Arm" except Tony was called "Mitts" and we didn't want another body part in the group. So, because of his affinity for cards—poker mostly—he had become Vito "the Ace."

"Anybody seen Mary Ann?" I asked.

Suddenly, Tony smiled. "She's here."

"Yeah," Vito said, slapping Tony on the back, "she came in with Tony, the lucky dog."

"Man," Sammy said, "she looks good, even if she ain't got an ass on her."

"You want to see her?" Tony's tone was anxious.

"Sure."

I agreed not only because he was so anxious to show her off. I was curious about what Mary Ann looked like after eighteen years.

"Come on." Tony took my arm in a grip of iron.

"See you guys . . ." I barely had time to say before he dragged me off.

I really had never gotten to know Mary Ann Grosso well in high school. I'd never gone out with her, although I knew a lot of guys who claimed they had. They all claimed to have scored, too, except for Tony. He said he never had, and no one else had, either.

He pulled me over to a table where a bunch of people were sitting. As we approached I was able to pick Mary Ann out with no problem. If anything, she was even more beautiful at thirty-six than she had been at eighteen. She had long dark hair that hung to her shoulders. Her eyebrows and eyelashes were very dark, and her eyes brown. I remembered that she had always had beautiful skin without a trace of acne, and she still did, smooth and pale.

She had been a lovely young girl, but she had grown up to become a truly beautiful woman.

"Mary Ann, here's Nick," Tony said. When she frowned he said, "Come on, you remember Nicky-D!"

"Of course. Nicky." I knew that she wasn't lying, she did remember me. She held out both hands and I took them. "It's good to see you."

"And you, Mary Ann. You look . . . wonderful."

"Don't she, though?" Tony blustered right over her soft "Thank you." He was obviously very proud of her, and when he told me that they were to be married, I realized why.

That was last week, when they were truly happy.

This week Mary Ann was dead.

2

After the service I decided not to accompany the family and friends to the cemetery. I stopped to tell Tony that and he grabbed my arm tightly.

"Come to Mary Ann's mother's house, Nick."

"Tony," I said, "I don't want to intrude . . ."

"Her mother wants you there, Nick. She wants to talk to you."

"I didn't think she'd even remember me."

"She doesn't. I told her you were a detective."

"Tony—"

"Please, Nick." His eyes were as pleading as his tone of voice.

"All right, Tony."

"Thanks, buddy." He was relieved. "We should be back at the house by two. Okay? There'll be lots of food."

"I'll be there."

He finally let go of my arm and I felt the blood starting to flow again.

I stood out in front of the funeral home and watched the procession of cars leave. I became aware then that someone was standing next to me.

"It's a damn shame, ain't it?" Vito asked. I hadn't seen him since the reunion, and hadn't noticed him inside.

"Yeah, it is." I looked at him. "I didn't see you inside."

"I didn't go in." He shook his head. "Couldn't. I didn't want to see her like that."

"Are you going to the house?"

"Nah." He shook his head again. "You?"

I nodded. "Tony asked me to."

"They're gonna hire you, ain't they?"

"I'm afraid they're going to try."

"Why afraid?"

"It's going to be hard turning them down."

"Why turn them down?"

"I don't investigate suicides, Vito."

"Then there's no problem, Nick." He slapped me on the

113

back. "She didn't kill herself."

"How do you know?"

"I knew her—I knew her as long and as well as Tony did. She'd never kill herself."

"Are you saying she was murdered?"

"I'm sayin' she didn't kill herself, Nick. That's *all* I'm sayin'."

"Vito—"

"Gotta go." He moved away from me abruptly. I watched him walk to the parking lot and get into a new Chevy. I realized that I didn't know what he did for a living. I don't think we ever talked about it at the reunion. I recalled talking to everyone else about what they were doing for a living, but now that I thought of it, Vito always seemed to avoid the subject. He seemed more willing to talk about the past, not the present.

I wondered if he'd meant to imply what I thought he'd been implying when he said he knew Mary Ann as well as Tony did?

I got to the house at two-thirty. It was in Bensonhurst, on Sixty-third Street. Actually, it was walking distance from my father's house, where I grew up.

"Nick," Tony Mitts said as I entered, "God." He came at me in the hall and clamped down on my arm again. "I'm glad you came."

"Take it easy, Tony—"

"I been trying to take it easy, Nick, but it ain't that simple. You don't *know* . . ."

"Don't know what, Tony?"

"Look, lemme tell Mary Ann's mother you're here, all right? Get somethin' to eat and I'll find you. Get a beer, 'kay?"

He was talking a mile a minute and he was gone before I could respond. I went looking for a beer and found one in the kitchen. I also found a girl crying. It took me a minute, but I recognized her as Grace, Mary Ann's sister. If I remembered correctly, Grace was about two years behind us in high school. She wasn't as pretty as her sister, but there was a resemblance, and she had the same smooth, pale skin.

She was sitting at the kitchen table, clutching a handkerchief and crying softly. I took a St. Paulie Girl from the refrigerator and turned to her.

"Grace?"

She looked up at me, hastily wiping away the moisture from her eyes. She frowned, trying to remember who I was.

"Grace, I'm Nick—"

"Delvecchio," she finished. "I remember. I had a terrible crush on you in high school." She blurted it out, and then clasped her hand over her mouth.

"Did you?" I asked. "I never knew that."

She took her hand away from her mouth and said, "Nobody did—only Mary Ann."

There was an awkward silence, which she broke.

"It's nice of you to come, Nick," she said. "I didn't think you'd remember . . . us."

"Well," I said, "I was at the reunion. I saw Mary Ann—"

"Wasn't she beautiful?" she asked, her eyes shining either from tears, or from pride. "Even more lovely than she was in high school?"

"Well, yes, she was," I said, not really knowing how to answer. I mean, what did she want me to say? She seemed to really mean it, but I had two older brothers, and I wasn't always so happy about that fact. Were there times, I wondered, when she didn't idolize her sister so much?

"I can't believe she's gone," Grace said, starting to sob

into her hanky. "Not . . . not like that."

It occurred to me then that I still didn't know exactly how Mary Ann had died.

"Nick, there you are," Tony said, bursting into the room. He didn't even seem to notice Grace. "Come on, Mary Ann's mother wants to talk to you."

"Grace," I said, "are you all right?"

"I'm fine, Nick," she said, waving her hand. "Go ahead, Mother wants you."

"Why don't we talk later? Huh?"

"Sure," she said with a little smile, "why not?"

"Come *on*, Nick!" Tony said, grabbing my arm.

Old friend or not, I was tired of having my arm mangled.

"Tony, take it *easy*, all right? I'm coming."

He released me like my flesh was hot and said, "Sorry."

"Lead the way."

I followed him down the hall.

3

Tony took me down a hallway past a couple of bedrooms to a room at the end. Inside, Mrs. Grosso was sitting on a bed, staring out the window. What was she seeing that no one else could see, I wondered.

From the looks of the room it was a girl's—most probably Mary Ann's. That was confirmed when I saw a framed photo on the dresser. It was Mary Ann and Tony, arms around each other, laughing. From the looks of the scene behind them it had been taken at Coney Island certainly during happier times. It also looked to be an older photo, not when they were in high school, but certainly not much later.

"Mrs. Grosso?" Tony said.

For a moment she didn't seem to hear him, and then she turned her head and looked at us. I wondered how old she was. Sixty? Sixty-five? She was still an attractive woman, obviously Mary Ann's and Grace's mother. She had the same skin: I remembered Tony telling me she had lost her husband about five years ago. And now Mary Ann. All she had left was her daughter Grace. No, check that. Let's say she *still* had Grace. That was something, wasn't it?

"Tony."

"This is Nick Delvecchio, Mrs. Grosso," Tony said, awkwardly. Obviously, even though he was going to marry her daughter, he hadn't gotten around to calling her anything more personal. "He went to school with us—"

"Yes," she said, "I know, Tony. I remember Nick. How's your father, Nick?"

"He's fine, Mrs. Grosso," I said.

"I see him at the store sometimes," she said. "He's gone through a lot, with the death of your brother and your sister being on that hijacked plane."

"He's come through it all with flying colors, Mrs. Grosso."

"Good, that's good," she said. "I came through my husband's death five years ago . . . but this . . . I don't know if I can come through this."

"You still have Grace, Mrs. Grosso."

"Yes," she said, "I still have Grace."

"Tell him about Mary Ann, Mrs. Grosso," Tony said, anxiously. "Tell him she didn't—"

"Tony," she said, interrupting him, "can I talk to Nick alone, please?"

He looked as if she had slapped him in the face.

"But—I thought—"

"Please, Tony?"

"Uh, well sure, Mrs. Grosso, sure . . ."

Tony gave me a puzzled glance, and then backed out of the room.

"Would you close the door, Nick?"

"Sure."

"And come and sit here by me," she said as I closed it. She patted the bed next to her and the folder, and when I sat the papers were between us.

"Please," she said, "call me Angela—it's actually Angelina, but that's too long, don't you think?"

"It's a pretty name."

"Yes. When I was in school—high school—they called me 'Angel.' Isn't that silly?"

"Mrs.—uh, Angela, can we talk about Mary Ann?"

"Of course. My Mary Ann," she said, "they say she killed herself."

"Who says so, Angela?"

"The police."

"Can you tell me how she died?"

"She died here," she said, touching the bed, "on this bed."

"But how did she die?"

"Pills," Angela Grosso said, "she took pills, that's what they say."

"Suicide."

Angela Grosso nodded.

"But Tony doesn't believe it."

"Tony was very much in love with Mary Ann, Nick. He refuses to believe it."

"And you?"

"Mary Ann was . . . troubled."

"Angela—"

"Here." She picked up the folder of papers and handed it to me.

"What are these?"

"Poems," she said, "my Mary Ann's poems."

"Poems," I said, puzzled.

"How well did you know my daughter, Nick?"

"Not well," I admitted. "We went to school together, but after we graduated I sort of lost touch—"

"Mary Ann wrote these poems," she said, patting the folder. "All these years since high school, she's written these poems. She even had some published in magazines."

"Really?" I said. "That's nice." I wasn't sure how to react. What did this have to do with anything?

"You don't understand," she said. "You have to read these poems to understand. The girl who wrote these poems—the *woman*—was . . . troubled."

"Mrs. Grosso, Tony said you wanted to talk to me—"

"I told him I didn't, Nick. He wants me to hire you to prove Mary Ann didn't commit suicide . . . but I believe she did. Read the poems, Nick, and you'll see."

"All right, Mrs. Grosso. I'll read them."

Tony was waiting when I came back down the hall.

"Did she hire you?"

"No, Tony, she didn't."

He firmed his jaw and said, "Then I want to, Nick. I want you to prove she didn't do it. Mary Ann wouldn't commit suicide. Those are her poems. They're beautiful. You read them and you'll see."

"I'll read them, Tony, and then I'll get back to you."

Angela Grosso thought the poems meant Mary Ann would commit suicide, and Tony thought they meant she couldn't. I was real curious about them now.

4

"So what did you tell him?" Sam asked.

We were in my apartment sharing a pizza which she had sprung for. It was her way of paying for information. She'd been waiting with the pizza when I got home from the Grosso house.

"What could I tell him?" I asked. "I took the poems and told him *and* her I'd read them."

She looked at the folder full of papers on the table, and then looked at me.

"Can I read them, too?"

Sam was a writer, mostly of romances as "Kit" Karson, but of late she had started writing mysteries, as well.

"Sure," I said. "After the pizza we'll start reading them."

"What did she say about them?"

"She said that once I read the poems I'd know that Mary Ann did kill herself."

"Her poems are supposed to tell you that?" Sam asked. "They must be pretty depressing poems."

"We'll find out," I said, picking up another slice of pizza, "after we eat."

There were dozens and dozens of poems—eighteen years' worth, according to Mary Ann's mother, but after reading half a dozen each Sam and I looked at each other, and then traded.

"Well?" I asked.

"God," she said, "these *are* depressing. The girl who wrote these was so . . . sad!"

I hated to admit it, but I agreed. Anyone who could write

"Angel of Death," "Last Request," and "Midnight Crisis," not to mention something called "Laying Down to Die," *was* more than just sad.

"I mean listen to this line from 'Midnight Crisis,' " Sam said, and then read aloud, " 'Raindrops kiss my black lapels, then weep into my chest.' " She looked at me and said, "It's so . . . beautiful, yet sad."

"You're a writer," I said. "Are these good?"

We were seated across from each other on the floor with the poems strewn out on the floor between us.

"These are . . . wonderful! I'm no poet, of course, but I think they're . . . well, wonderful."

"But sad," I said, "so sad."

"Maybe not all sad. Listen to this line from 'Laying Down to Die.' 'She's blind to the jelly bean colors, of balloons on a turquoise sky.' "

"That's great, but does it mean she did or did not kill herself?"

"I don't know, but try this. What if writing it down, writing down all of the sadness she felt, was her way of dealing with it, of getting it out. What if she *wrote* it to keep from committing suicide. It could have been some sort of rite of expiation on her part."

"If you're gonna flaunt something can you make it something other than your writer's vocabulary? Like maybe your body?"

She made a face at me. "All that means is what I just said."

"That writing it down would prevent her from having to commit suicide—uh, in her own mind, I mean."

"Right."

I looked down at the poems on the floor, moved them around some, and then heaved a big sigh.

"What?" Sam asked.

"I don't buy it, Sam," I said. "I think she took her own life."

"So what are you going to do?"

"Ask some questions," I said. "Maybe if I can find out why, I can put her mother's mind to rest."

"But you're not going to treat it like a murder?"

"I can't," I said. "I just don't see it that way."

"Well . . . it's not as if you couldn't investigate it that way. I mean, as far as the police are concerned it's a closed case, so you wouldn't be stepping on their toes."

I looked at her and asked, "You think somebody killed her? By making her take pills?"

She shrugged. "Maybe somebody poisoned her."

I shook my head.

"You're getting too involved in this mystery-writing thing," I said. "You're seeing conspiracies where there just ain't any."

"All right," she said, getting to her feet. She was wearing a big floppy sweatshirt and a pair of jeans. Her feet were bare, since she'd only had to walk over from across the hall. I noticed—and not for the first time—that she had pretty feet. Her toes weren't all gnarly like some women's were.

"All right what?"

"Look into it any way you want," she said. "As long as you look into it."

"I'm only going to look into it at all because I couldn't tell Tony no," I said.

"Isn't he still your friend?"

"I don't know," I said, honestly. "Before the reunion I hadn't seen him in years."

"I have to go," Sam said, "I have to do twenty pages tonight."

"Has all of this talk about murder inspired you?" I asked.

On the way to the door she said, "As a matter of fact, it has. I'll be up past midnight, in case you want to talk, or get a snack."

"I'll let you know," I said, staring down at the poems on the floor.

"Read some more, Nicky," she said from the door. "Maybe you'll find one that will tell you something definite."

She went out the door, closing it behind her. I already knew something definite. Mary Ann Grosso was one depressed person for a long time.

What I wanted to find out was why?

I read some more, but at one point I just had to stop. Jesus, *I* was getting depressed, and I'm normally a real happy fella. Ask anybody.

I put the poems away and went to bed before midnight. Let Sam get her own snack.

5

The next morning I got up—late—and leafed through the poems again, but I didn't have the heart to start reading. I left them in my desk and decided to talk to people who knew Mary Ann Grosso a lot better than I did.

I started with Grace. I called her at home, caught her there and asked her to have lunch with me. She agreed, but told me to come to the house at noon and she'd make something. That left me an hour to work with. I decided to check in with the police and see what they had on Mary Ann Grosso. I made some phone calls, invoked the name of a friend, and managed to pry this out of the detective who caught the case: there were no signs of violence on the body. That meant that no one had held her down and forced her to swallow the pills.

She seemed to have simply taken the pills and laid down to die, the detective said. There was no question about it in anyone's mind but that she committed suicide.

"Did they find a pill container?"

"Yes. There was one in the downstairs bathroom on the sink. It was the mother's. The daughter must have taken the pills, left it there, and walked to the bed. And then there was the note."

"What note?" I was about a second away from hanging up when he said this.

"The one they found clutched in her hand."

"Which one?"

"I don't know," the man said, "it had something to do with suicide."

"Wait a minute," I said, and pulled out the folder. I went through the poems one by one and then found one with suicide in the title.

"That's the one," the detective said when I read the title to him. "She had it in her hand."

Her mother hadn't told me that.

"Thanks," I said, and hung up.

There was a knock on the door and I opened it to find Sam standing in the hall.

"What are you doing up?" I asked. "I thought you did twenty pages last night."

"I did, but I wanted to see if you'd read any more of the poems."

"I'm reading one now," I said, waving it. "Listen to this. 'Eyelids covering forever her pain, Beating heart eternally resting.' She had it in her hand when she died."

"Which one is it?"

"It's called 'Suicidal Daydreams,' " I said. "Whataya think of that?"

★ ★ ★ ★ ★

When I got to the Grosso house Grace had soup and sandwiches waiting. She also looked as if she had dressed for a date. I hoped I hadn't given her the wrong idea. Actually, she looked very pretty . . .

"Nick," she said, "Tony told me he . . . he hired you."

"He thinks he hired me," I said, and she looked puzzled. "I'm not going to bill him, Grace."

"Well . . . that's nice of you . . . but what can you do for him . . . us?"

"I don't know," I said. "Do you feel the way he does about Mary Ann's death, or do you agree with your mother?"

She opened her mouth to answer, but her voice failed her. There were two glasses of water on the table. She took a sip from one, either because her mouth was dry, or because she was buying time to think.

"I don't know how I feel, Nick," she said, finally. "I mean, sometimes I'm just absolutely numb."

"Do you feel that someone might have killed your sister?"

"My God," she said, shaking her head. She held her hands up, as if to cup her head between them, but instead she just held them there. "It sounds ludicrous when you say it out loud. Who'd want to kill Mary Ann? And why?"

She reached out suddenly and grabbed my hand.

"Nick, do you think someone killed my sister?"

"No, Grace, I don't," I said. "I'm sorry, but I believe she committed suicide."

I took "Suicidal Daydreams" from my pocket and held it out to her.

"What's this?"

"This is the poem they found in her hand. The police consider it a suicide note."

She unfolded the page and read it, then let her right hand

125

drop to the table, holding the poem loosely.

"Do you know when she wrote that?"

Her face reddened.

"Grace . . ."

"Yes."

"When?"

She touched her forehead with her left hand, as if she had a headache.

"Grace?" I made my voice firmer.

"A couple of years ago," she said, finally.

"Did she talk about suicide then?"

She lifted her eyes then to look at me. They were shining with tears.

"It's not about suicide, Nick."

"Come on," I said, "look at the title. What else could it be about?"

"Look at the last line of the first stanza." She spread the poem out on the table.

"'Damaged goods denied final blessing,' " I read.

"And the second stanza."

I looked at the last line of the second stanza and read, " 'Remains of a deadly assault.' "

"Don't you see?" she asked. " 'Damaged goods'? 'Deadly assault'?"

"What are you telling me, Grace?"

"Nick . . ."

Suddenly it came to me. I realized what she was talking about.

"Grace . . . are you telling me Mary Ann was raped? That's what this is about?"

She nodded, the tears now streaming down her face.

"When? By who?"

"She never told anyone," she said, "anyone but me."

"Why not?" I asked. "Why didn't you tell your mother?"

Her eyes widened. "Oh God, Nick, she could never have told Mother. She would have thought . . . Mary Ann was dirty."

"No," I said, "your mother would have helped her—"

"You don't know my mother, Nick," Grace said. "If she ever found out about this it would have disgraced her. She would have . . . would have . . ."

Have what? I wondered. Whatever she was thinking she couldn't say out loud.

"Nick, haven't you wondered why Tony and Mary Ann are just getting—*were* just getting married now? After all these years?"

"Well . . . yeah, I wondered . . . a little . . ."

"Mary Ann's led a kind of wild life, Nick," Grace said. "She's not—wasn't—the nice little Catholic girl that . . . well, she's not . . ."

She was going to say, ". . . the nice little Catholic girl that I am."

"She's been . . . promiscuous in the past, but now she was ready to settle down, and Tony—he's loved her all these years, and he was ready to take her."

"Who was it?" I asked. "Did she tell you that?"

She nodded.

"She told me," Grace said, "but . . . do you think he killed her? I mean, that was two years ago and she . . . she forgave him, Nick. Can you imagine? So why would he kill her now?"

"I don't know, Grace." I said. "Why don't you let me go and ask him."

6

Vito Pricci lived in the old neighborhood, not far from where Mary Ann lived, and where my father now lives. From there I walked to Vito's house.

Actually, it was Vito's father's house, but Vito lived there now, since both his parents had passed away. He had no brothers and sisters, which was unusual for someone of our generation. When I was a kid I didn't have many friends who were only children. That's what happens when you grow up Catholic and Italian.

I didn't know if Vito would be there or not, but I hoped he would, because I wanted to be able to wrap this case up quickly. I just found the whole thing too . . . depressing.

So I was hopeful when I rang his doorbell.

"Nick," he said, showing surprise. "What are you—it's good to see you."

"Can I talk to you, Vito?"

"Well . . . well, sure, come on in." He backed away to let me enter.

He closed the door behind us and led me into the living room. The house was very much like Mary Ann's, and very much like my father's. It's funny, I grew up in my father's house. It was my home for almost twenty years, and yet I always thought of it as my father's house.

"Can I get you a beer?" he asked. "Or something?"

"No, nothing, Vito. I just want to talk."

"About what?"

"About Mary Ann."

He frowned. "What about her? Did you find out that she didn't commit suicide?"

"No," I said, "I didn't find that out, but I found out other things."

He shuffled his feet uncomfortably and asked, "Uh, what other things?"

"Come on, Vito," I said. "I think you know what other things."

He shook his head slightly and said, "Uh, Nick, I don't know—"

"I know about the rape, Vito."

"What?" he said, his eyes widening. "No, whoa, wait a minute, there wasn't no rape, Nicky. I don't know who you been talking to—"

"I've been talking to someone Mary Ann confided in, Vito."

"Jesus," he said, touching his face, "she didn't tell Tony that, did she?"

"I think if she had told Tony you'd know it, Vito—you would have known it two years ago, when it happened. He would have killed you."

"Nick," he said, "wait, let me show you something. All right? Before you say anything else."

Vito went into the dining room. He went to a hutch and opened a drawer. Just for a moment I wondered if he was going to come out with a gun, but instead he took a folded-up piece of paper and carried it back to me, leaving the drawer open.

"Here."

"What's this?"

"A poem," he said. "Mary Ann wrote it . . . for me. Read it."

I unfolded the paper and read the title, "You." I read the first stanza and saw that it was Mary Ann's, all right. I mean, I was starting to recognize her style.

"Disappointments in life are many." It was three stanzas, and the third finished with the lines, "Now I will be forever changed, refreshed, from loving you."

I looked at him. "Did she write this before the rape, or after, Vito?"

Vito stared at me for a few seconds, and his eyes widened

again. He said, horrified—and if he was acting he was damned good!—"Jesus, you think I killed her!"

"Tell me what happened, Vito."

"Nick . . . look . . . I've loved Mary Ann for years, man. Ever since high school. You know those stories we used to hear, about guys who scored with her?"

"Tony said they weren't true," I remembered.

"Well, they were. I mean, I loved her, too, but I wasn't blind like he was. He refused to believe the stories, but I knew they were true."

I didn't know what to say. If what Grace said was true about Mary Ann's promiscuity, then it probably *had* started in high school.

"So, what does that mean, that she deserved—"

"No, you don't understand," he said, "just listen." There was a look of desperation on his face, and in his eyes. "Tony wanted to marry her right out of high school, but she wasn't ready for that. She wanted to live her life, you know? Sow her wild oats and all that? She traveled, she had affairs, but she always came back home. Tony and her mother, they kept treating her like she was a saint, but I knew different.

"I was always here, too, Nick, and always in love with her. Then, about three years ago, she came home and she was different. It was like she found God, or something, you know? After all these years? Like all of a sudden she *was* the saint Tony and her mother thought she was—but not quite. Even though she started to see Tony regularly, and they talked about marriage, all of a sudden she noticed me, you know? It was like a high school dream come true for me. We talked, we went places together, we did things . . . but she'd never have sex with me. I couldn't understand that. She always told me I was the one who was keeping her sane, who knew her for what she was and still loved her. Tony, she said, loved who he

130

thought she was, and her mother—well, Angelina would never believe anything bad about her little Mary Ann."

"But she wouldn't come across, huh?"

"It wasn't like that." He wiped away the sweat on his forehead with his palm. "I didn't want a quick fuck, I wanted to love her, marry her. I couldn't understand why she wouldn't make love to me."

"So you got tired of waiting?"

"Damn it, you don't understand!" he shouted. "She came over one day and she gave me that poem, said she'd written it for me. I was overwhelmed. Nobody'd ever done anything like that for me before. She . . . she let me kiss her, and then . . . then when things started to heat up, she pushed me away . . . but she didn't push very hard, you know? I felt if I pressed her, if I insisted . . . and before you knew it we were on the floor . . . okay, so I tore her clothes a little, but . . . but I wouldn't call it rape, Nick. I'd *never* call it rape!"

"But she did, right?"

"Yeah," he said. Suddenly, it was as if he lost all the strength in his legs. He sank into a chair and said, "Yeah, she did . . . but you know what? She said she forgave me. She understood."

"And?"

"And she said she never wanted to see me again . . . not like that. She said we were finished, even as friends."

"And you took that?"

"Sure, I took it," he said. "I loved her, I'd never hurt her."

I stared at him. I didn't know what had happened between them that day. She called it rape, and he didn't. Who knew? She told her sister Grace it was rape, and she was too ashamed to ever tell her mother.

He looked up at me with anguished eyes. "I didn't kill her, Nicky. I loved her. I always loved her. Why would I kill her

131

two years later, huh? Tell me that?"

I couldn't. It didn't make sense. He wouldn't wait two years and then become angry enough to kill her. So then the question became who *would* become angry enough to kill her if they found this out?

Vito hung his head and said, "I didn't kill her, Nick . . . I didn't . . . I didn't . . ."

I believed him.

7

From Vito's house I went back to Mary Ann's mother's house to close the whole thing out.

Grace answered the door and looked at me with surprise.

"Is there something you forgot to ask me?"

"No, Grace," I said, stepping inside, "I'm here to talk to your mother."

"She's in Mary Ann's room," she said, closing the door.

"Tell me something, Grace. Did Mary Ann use sleeping pills?"

"Mary Ann?" Grace shook her head. "Mary Ann slept like a top, Nick. She slept like . . . oh . . ."

She'd been about to say, "Like the dead."

"Is there a medicine cabinet in the downstairs bathroom?"

"No, only in the upstairs. Why, Nick?"

"We'll talk before I leave, okay?"

"Sure."

I went down the hall and found Angela Grosso sitting on Mary Ann's bed, just the way I had left her the day before.

"Angela?"

For a moment it seemed as if she didn't hear me, like the day before, then she turned her head and looked at me.

"Nick," she said, "what is it?"

"I want to talk."

"Come in," she said, "sit."

"No," I said, shying away from the bed, "I'd rather stand, Angela."

She frowned. "Well, all right."

"Tell me about Mary Ann, Angela."

"What about her?"

"What kind of child was she?"

She got a faraway look in her eyes and said, "She was a beautiful child, beautiful. So obedient when she was younger . . ."

"And then what happened? When did she change? Was it in junior high school? Or high school? When did she change exactly, Angela?"

"Change?"

"You know what I mean," I said. "When did she start . . . going boy crazy."

"Boy crazy? Nick, who have you been talking to?"

"Not that many people, Angela," I said. "I've read her poetry, and I talked to Grace . . . and to Vito."

"Vito . . ."

"You know about Vito, don't you, Angela? You know about a lot of things."

She remained silent.

I moved closer and said, "Tell me about Mary Ann, Angelina. Tell what she was like."

She waited a long time to answer, and I waited with her. I didn't want to hear any more of that "beautiful child" stuff, and if the truth was going to come out, I was willing to wait for it.

Finally she looked at me and her expression was different. No longer was she the mother in mourning, now she wore the expression of a dissatisfied mother, a long-suffering mother.

"She was disrespectful," she said, slowly, "she was . . . bad . . . a trial, Nick, believe me. She was . . . wild. Everyone thought she was such a saint."

"Who's everyone, Angelina?"

"My friends, who else?" she said. "They all told me what a good daughter I had, how lucky I was. They didn't know how she *really* was. When she discovered boys and . . . sex!" She said "sex" as if it had four letters, not three. "She had sex for—the first time in junior high school. Did you know that?"

I didn't know that, but what could I say?

"She was . . . uncontrollable," she went on, "and she was smart, so smart. I mean, she fooled my friends, and she fooled a lot of her own friends. She fooled Tony . . . oh, she fooled him completely."

"But not you, huh?" I asked. "And not Vito."

"Vito," she said, shaking her head. "What she did to that poor boy."

"What she did to him?" I asked.

She looked at me. "You have found out a lot of things, haven't you?"

"Yes, ma'am, I have."

"You know about the . . . the rape?"

"Yes, I do."

She shook her head and made a disgusted sound with her mouth.

"There was no rape," she said, staring back out the window. "Vito was probably the only man who gave her what she really wanted."

"Why was she marrying Tony, then?"

"Why? Because she said she changed, that's why. She came back from . . . wherever she was and claimed she had changed. She'd seen the light. She actually said that." She looked at me again. "After making my life miserable for years, *she* saw the light. She was going to marry Tony and settle down. Poor Tony, he waited years for her."

"Angelina," I said, "when did she tell you about the rape?"

"The night she died," she answered without hesitation, "she said she had some things to tell me, to get off her chest. That's what she said. She told me things I knew already, things she didn't think I knew. Things she did that . . . that no Catholic girl should ever hear, let alone do."

She averted her eyes. She didn't look at me, or out the window; she looked instead at a crucifix that was hanging on the wall.

"I knew what she was like, Nick. In junior high school, in high school and . . . and after, as an adult. Did you know that she wasn't at her father's funeral? Couldn't be bothered to come back for it. What kind of daughter is that? Tell me."

"That was then, Angelina," I said, wanting to keep her on the track. "What about now?"

"She thought she could change, but I knew better," she said, as if she hadn't heard me. "I knew she'd never change. She'd make my life miserable again, and she'd do the same to Tony. She'd hurt both of us."

"So you killed her?"

Her head whipped around and she glared at me.

"I did not!" she snapped. "She was my daughter, for God's sake."

"Angela, the police found a pill container in the downstairs bathroom. They were yours."

"She must have taken them."

"Your girls never went into your bathroom, Angela, remember?" I asked. "Even as adults they thought of it as your bathroom." The way I thought of my father's house as "his" house.

"She could have gone in, and taken them, when no one was home," she said, lamely.

"Why would she take them from the upstairs bathroom, and then go downstairs to ingest them? And then leave the container on the sink instead of doing it all in her room?"

"I . . . I don't know. She must have taken them."

"Did she, Angela?" I asked. "Did she do that? Or did you give them to her?"

She hesitated, then said, "I did not *make* her take them."

"But you gave them to her, right?"

She looked at me, then away, back at the crucifix.

"I didn't know what to do," she said. "I . . . prayed for guidance. If she stayed here, if she got married and stayed here, eventually people would find out . . . what kind of person she was."

"What if she really had changed, though?" I asked. "What about that? What if she just wanted to marry Tony and live a normal life as his wife?"

"She wouldn't . . ." She shook her head. "She couldn't . . ."

"Maybe not, Angela, maybe not, but she deserved the chance to try, don't you think? Or was it more important that your friends didn't find out what a . . . a trial she was, that your oldest daughter was not the saint they thought she was?"

"She couldn't change," she said. "She just couldn't. I had to convince her of that."

"Is that what you did, then?" I asked. "You convinced her that she couldn't change, and that she might as well die?"

There was no answer.

"You went and got the pills, and you gave them to her," I said. "Did you sit and watch while she took them, Angela? Did you wait for your daughter to die, and then arrange her on the bed with the poems?"

She glared at me. "What kind of a mother do you think I am?"

I stared at her, unsure what she was talking about. Was I being criticized for thinking she'd kill Mary Ann, or that she'd sit there and watch her daughter die?

"I think you're a selfish mother, Angelina."

"You don't understand. Your father, he'd understand. He's gone through a lot—"

"He's gone through plenty," I said, interrupting her, "but he'd never take away the chance any of his children had for happiness. You did that to Mary Ann, didn't you, Angelina? You took away the one chance she did have to change."

"She couldn't have changed," she insisted, shaking her head violently. Now who was she trying to convince, me or herself?

"Well, we'll never know, will we, Angela? You saw to that."

I moved close and bent over. "Did you actually tell your own daughter she'd be better off dead than trying to change?"

"I did what I thought . . . was right . . ."

"Well, what will people think now, Angela?" I asked. "What will they think if this gets out?"

She looked at me again then, with fear in her eyes for the first time.

"You'll tell—"

"I won't tell," I said. "I can't tell the police. Even if you did convince her to take the pills, you're right, you didn't *force* her. Besides, I can't prove it. Only you and I know about it, right? How could I prove it?"

"I did the right thing," she said, more to herself than me—or was it to God. "I did the right thing, I know it!"

"She was your daughter, Angelina," I said. "No matter what she did to you—or what you imagine she did—the right

137

thing would have been to help her."

I started to leave, then turned. "Did it ever occur to you that by actually taking the pills that you gave her, by doing what you wanted her to do, she demonstrated that she *had* changed?"

She looked at me then and there was no fear or puzzlement in her eyes. What I saw there was horror.

What if I was right, she must have been thinking. What then?

I left her there, sitting on her dead daughter's bed, and went down the hall. I wondered if I would have done that, left her there like that, if the container she was holding was full instead of empty.

There was nothing else I could do. Mary Ann Grosso had killed herself, she had taken the pills by her own hand and committed suicide. That was a fact I couldn't change. If she'd been stronger—maybe if she'd been the person she used to be—she wouldn't have done it, but maybe in one last-ditch effort to please her mother she had downed those pills and laid down on the bed with her poems, laid down to die . . .

"Nick?" Grace said as I came down the stairs. She was staring at me with a million questions in her eyes. Why, I thought then, why should Angelina and I be the only two to know?

"Grace," I said, putting my hand out to her, "let's talk . . ."

Acknowledgement

Every title and line of poetry used in this story were written by Marthayn Pelegrimas. The story is that much better for it. My thanks to her for allowing me to use them.

A Favor for Sam

1

"Sam! You're a day early. You weren't due back from Chicago until tomorrow."

She was sitting on the floor with her back against my door as I came down the hall. She was wearing a T-shirt, and she was barefoot.

"Oh, Nick!" She started to cry.

I stared at her, unsure what to say, so I slid down and sat next to her. She looked at me and then wiped an errant tear as it worked its way down her face.

"Lisa's my friend . . . a writer who I see at these conventions. When she didn't arrive I called her and . . . and she told me on the phone that she tested positive for . . . for the HIV virus."

She was talking very fast, the way people who are upset do. I'd never seen her this upset. She just about collapsed in my arms and started sobbing. You have to understand about my neighbor, Samantha Karson. She's smart, gorgeous, sensitive, and confident. I'd never seen her cry before.

"And . . . and that's not the worst part. She really loved this guy, Nick, the guy who . . . who gave it to her. At first she didn't want to believe that she got it from him, but there was no one else."

"Did she confront him?"

"On the phone. She called him and told him that she had

AIDS, and do you know what the son of a bitch said to her?"

"What?"

"He told her it was her fault, that she should have been more careful."

"What? He gave her AIDS, and *she* should have been careful?"

"That's what he said."

"What a shit."

"He also said it wasn't his responsibility to tell her."

"Then whose was it?"

"He told her that she should just treat everybody like they have AIDS."

"That's good advice—funny, too, coming from him. What kind of shape is she in?"

"She said she's on some kind of medication and she's responding well to it, but you know that will only put the inevitable off for a while. She's going to die, Nick."

"I'm sorry, Sam."

"There's something else."

"There's more?"

Sam nodded.

"She found out from another girl that the same guy gave her AIDS."

"Before or after your friend?"

"Before. She was his girlfriend before Lisa."

"Too bad Lisa didn't meet her earlier."

"I feel terrible. I wish there was something I could do."

"Like what?"

Sam shrugged. "I don't know. Something."

"Well, I wish there was something I could do to help you, Sam."

Sam looked at me sharply and said, "There is."

I looked back at her and asked, "Did I just walk into that

with my eyes wide open?"

"Nick, Lisa wants to confront the guy—face-to-face."

"So?"

"She doesn't know where he is. She can't find him."

"I repeat. So?"

"You could find him. You're good at that."

"Sam—"

She stopped me by putting her hand on my arm.

"Please, Nick. There's so little that can be done for her. If she could confront him . . ."

"Aw, Sam . . ."

She kept staring at me, her eyes pleading. How could I turn her down? And what would it cost me to try? It would probably make *her* feel like she was doing something, which would make her feel better.

"Okay, Sam, I'll see what I can do. Where does your friend live?"

"St. Louis."

"Saint—Okay, well, where does the guy—what's his name—live?"

"His name is Ted and he lives in St. Louis, too."

She had a wary look on her face, like she was waiting for me to explode.

"St. Louis? Sam, that's in Missouri. That's all I know about St. Louis—"

"What do you have to know? If you're looking for a missing person, don't you do the same things, no matter where he lives? Check his home, his work, and . . . and whatever else you check?"

"Well, sure, but I don't know my way around St. Louis—"

"Lisa said she can tell you how to get anyplace you want to go."

"Lisa said—you already told her I would come?"

"Well . . . you don't think I expected you to pay your own airfare, do you?"

2

Sam said her friend Lisa didn't have much money but she did have enough to pay for airfare from New York to St. Louis. Of course, I had to lay out the two hundred and forty-eight dollars and she'd reimburse me later. Oh, and Sam said there was a catch—she was coming, too. She said she wanted to spend some time with Lisa. Since I considered that I was doing the whole thing as a favor to Sam, I didn't argue as long as she did what she was going to do while I did what I was going to do. She agreed.

Lisa Carlson lived in a suburb of St. Louis called Shrewsbury. Well, they didn't call them suburbs, they called them cities. That meant that within the city of St. Louis were these other little cities such as Shrewsbury, Webster Groves, Clayton, and others. Being from New York, it was confusing to me, so I preferred to think of them as suburbs, or even boroughs.

We rented a car at the St. Louis Airport, which was the biggest airport I'd ever been in. One entire section of it was the TWA hub and we seemed to walk miles before we left the gate area and got into the area with the ticket counters, shops, and transportation.

When we got in the car I got behind the wheel and asked Sam where we were going. That's when she explained about all the little cities and told me the one Lisa lived in.

"How do we get there?"

"She gave me directions."

She started telling me about I-270, and something called the inner belt, that was also known as I-170, and then there was Highway 44—I let her get that far and stopped her.

"I'll drive," I said, "and you just point."

"Okay."

With her pointing we only went the wrong way twice but we finally ended up in Shrewsbury, getting off the highway at a street called Laclede Station Boulevard. Lisa lived in an apartment complex on Big Bend Road, and when she opened the door to greet us she and Sam embraced warmly. Lisa seemed genuinely touched by Sam's presence, and at that point I was glad I was helping both of them.

Sam made the introductions and then we sat down at Lisa's table with coffee and cookies and I took a good look at her. Outwardly there were no indications of the disease. She was slender and attractive, with brown eyes and long dark hair.

"You can't see it," she said to me.

"Oh, I'm sorry." I thought I'd been staring and she caught me.

"It's all right. Actually, I don't have AIDS, I simply tested positive for the HIV virus."

"But that will become AIDS, won't it?" Sam asked.

"Maybe," Lisa said, biting her bottom lip, then, "probably. It depends on how well I continue to respond to the medication."

We were silent for a while and when it became awkward, Lisa broke it herself.

"I'm glad you came here to help me, Nick. What do you need?"

"Well, Sam says the guy's name is Ted. I need his full name, his home address, where he works, who his friends are—if you know them—and some other women he might have seen."

"His name's Ted Drew. I can write down his address for

you. I know the last place he worked, but I don't think he works there anymore. Um, I know one or two of his friends, but I don't know their addresses."

"Maybe you could give me some idea where they hang out."

"Sure, I can do that. As for other women, there's his former girlfriend—"

"Sam mentioned her. I definitely want to talk to her."

"I have her address and phone number. We're kind of, uh, well, members of the same club."

"What condition is she in, Lisa?"

"She's showing some signs, Nick. She's lost a lot of weight."

"What about medication?"

Lisa looked down.

"She was on the same medication I am. It worked for a while, but now she's getting worse."

"And how about Ted? What kind of shape is he in?"

"The last time I saw him you couldn't tell he had anything wrong with him."

I frowned at that. What kind of justice was there when he could go around infecting innocent, trusting women and not be suffering himself. AIDS is not something I know a lot about. Okay, I'm ignorant, like a lot of other people. I know that safe sex is advised, and I've had those kinds of conversations with women, but I didn't know that someone could have it, pass it on, and not show any sign themselves.

That sucked.

"Why don't you write all that information down for me, and anything else you think might be helpful?"

"All right."

Sam and I waited, drinking coffee and munching without

appetite on cookies, while Lisa got a lined pad and wrote for almost ten minutes.

"There." She stopped writing and pushed the pad to me. I tore off the sheet, scanned it, folded it, and put it away.

"I want to ask you something, Lisa."

"All right."

"Do you think Ted is deliberately infecting women with this AIDS virus?"

"Well, he knew he had it when he slept with Kitty—that was his girlfriend before me—and then when he and I were together. I guess that means it's deliberate."

"If that's the case," Sam said, "he could be brought up on charges."

"No, what I mean is, is he the kind of man who is looking to infect as many women as he can on purpose?"

She frowned.

"That would make him . . . evil."

"I guess it would."

She thought for a moment, then shook her head slowly.

"I really don't know, Nick."

"That's okay." I stood up. "I'd better get started. Do you have any pictures of Ted?"

"I thought you might ask."

I'd noticed when we arrived that she was limping slightly. Now she limped over to the counter and took a picture from where she'd left it. Coming back she saw me looking at her.

"I stepped on a nail a couple of days back. Here."

It was a wallet-sized head shot. Drew was a good-looking man in his late thirties, brown hair falling down over his forehead. I could see where a woman might want to brush the hair back, maybe run her fingers through it. He was smiling, looking for all the world like Beaver Cleaver all grown-up. The All American boy, passing AIDS along like a bad joke.

Before I left, I came up with one more question.

"How long has it been since you saw him?"

"The day I told him I tested positive was the last time I saw him. That was about a month ago."

I walked to the door with Sam, followed by Lisa. I opened the front door and walked out, then turned and saw that Sam was still inside.

"Come on," I said, "we have to get a hotel room."

"Oh, we do?"

"Well, sure . . ."

"One room?"

"Well . . . it would be cheaper that way, wouldn't it?" I have to admit, the prospect of sharing a room with Sam was . . . interesting.

"I suppose it would, but I have a better idea."

"What?"

She smiled and said, "Get my bag out of the car. I'm staying here with Lisa."

"You had this planned all along, didn't you?"

She just smiled, so I got her bag from the car, gave it to her, and told her I'd call when I got to a hotel.

3

I found a Best Western nearby, off of Highway 44, and checked in. In my room I took out Lisa's sheet of paper and read it. I had gotten a map of St. Louis from the car rental, so I spent the next fifteen minutes finding addresses and marking routes in pen. Before I left the room I called Sam and told her where I was staying.

"Why don't you come back here for dinner?" she suggested.

I agreed, and we planned for me to arrive at six.

The first person I wanted to see was Kitty Marks, Ted Drew's former girlfriend. I had her phone number and called her. She had spoken with Lisa and said I could come right over. She lived in Brentwood and since I had her on the phone I asked the best and most direct route to her. Armed with that, I got to her apartment in twenty minutes.

Her illness was obvious because she was at least five feet ten and seriously underweight. There were also hollows beneath her eyes. Her hair was dirty blond, almost brown, and listless. She kept her arms folded, with her elbows in the palms of her hands. I noticed that her right hand was bandaged.

"I can't tell you much," she said, "except that the son of a bitch gave me AIDS."

"I hope you'll excuse me if I ask you how you know it was him."

"I was with only him for six months, Mr. Delvecchio."

"Nick, please." Even as I spoke it sounded inane to me. I'd probably never see this girl again in my life—or hers.

"Nick . . . and before that I hadn't been with anyone over eight months."

"Did you or he have an AIDS test before you seeing each other?"

"I mentioned it, but he refused. He said how could I claim to love him and think he wasn't clean?" She looked ashamed. "I bought it."

"After you found you had AIDS did you tell him?"

"You bet I did. You know what the bastard did?"

"What?"

"He moved out the same day. Quit his job and moved out."

"Did he express . . . remorse? Say he was sorry—"

"He said I should have been more careful."

Same thing he said to Lisa.

"You know what pisses me off? He's probably out there right now giving it to some other poor unsuspecting girl. I'd like to cut off his dick!"

I couldn't blame her for that.

"Can you give me some idea of where to find him? Who he hung out with?"

"I can tell you who he hung out with when we were together, but I don't know where he goes now."

"That'll be good enough."

I left Kitty Marks's place with a couple of more hangouts I could try in my search for Ted Drew.

I went from her house to the home address I had for Ted. It was an apartment complex on Manchester Road. I knocked on the door, but no one answered. I went to the office to find out if he still lived there. The woman there told me he didn't, because he was two months behind in the rent. Even if he returned, she said, he wouldn't get back in. I asked if he had left anything behind and she said no. She added that the apartment was furnished, so the furniture wasn't his. I thanked her and left.

My next stop was the place where he was working while he was seeing Lisa. It was a print shop, and when I asked for him the owner angrily told me that Ted had simply stopped coming in, with no notice at all.

I left there and stopped at a Hardee's to eat. There are no Hardee's in New York, but there are Roy Rogers, and since Hardee's owns Roy's, I tried the fried chicken and found it the same. I think Roy's has better chicken than KFC.

Over my lunch I thought about Ted Drew. Why would a man who has a disease make the conscious decision to spread it? Did he figure he'd gotten it from a woman, so he was trying to pay all women back? As I understood AIDS it was statistically more likely that a woman would get it from a man than the other way around. Also, the people most susceptible to contracting AIDS were gays and drug users. I'd have to call Lisa and ask her if Ted used drugs.

The fact that Drew had abandoned both his home and his job fit the man's pattern. When he found out that Kitty tested positive, he moved out and quit his job. Lisa hadn't been living with him, but he left his apartment anyway and stopped going to his job, in effect quitting.

How far back did this pattern go? I wondered. Did he sleep with women until they tested positive, then move, quit his job, and start over? Was he doing this all over St. Louis? If he did it long enough, wasn't he bound to run into an old girlfriend or boss?

Since he'd infected two women I knew of, I wondered if Ted Drew hadn't already left town, moved to another city where he could start fresh with new victims.

Jesus, I thought, if women started dying because he was infecting them, did that make him a serial killer?

4

I hit a couple of bars where Drew hung out when he was with Kitty Marks. I didn't see any way around asking for him. I didn't have the time to start staking places out, waiting for him to show up.

I tried to be casual about it, but bartenders these days are a suspicious bunch. As soon as you say, "Hey, Ted Drew been around lately?" they want to know who you are and where you're from. If you happen to tell them that you owe him money and want to find him, that's the end of it. They shut up. You're better off saying that he owes you money.

In the third place I caught a bartender's interest.

"Owes you money, huh?"

"Yep."

"A lot?"

I played with my Busch bottle and said, "Enough to make me want to find him."

"Gambling, huh?"

I looked him in the eye and said, "He picks the wrong teams."

"Don't I know it. You're shit out of luck, pal. He already owes a couple of regulars money and he don't come here no more."

"Any idea where he does hang out?"

He didn't mince words. "What's it worth to you?"

"You sell the information to your regulars, too?"

"Fuck them. He owes them forty, fifty bucks from a one-night bet. They ain't making book."

He assumed I had booked bets for Drew, and consequently figured that Drew was into me for a lot.

"I'll go ten."

"Make it twenty."

"Fifteen."

"Twenty, and I think I can tell you where to find him."

We matched stares for a while, and then I gave in.

"Okay, twenty."

"Let's see it."

See? What'd I tell you. A suspicious lot. I handed him the twenty.

"Check the Landing. I heard from a guy that he saw Drew down there."

"What landing?"

"Laclede's Landing, by the river."

"What river?"

"Where you from, pal? The Mississippi."

Yep, that was a river, all right.

I got back to Lisa's place at six. She and Sam had prepared dinner and while we ate I told them what I'd been doing. When we were done Lisa gave me directions to Laclede's Landing.

"A lot of people hang out down there," she added. "There are lots of clubs and restaurants and you can walk along the river."

"The Mississippi," I said to Sam.

She gave me a funny look and said, "I know."

Sam wanted to come to the Landing with me, but I vetoed the idea. I figured when I found Ted Drew he wasn't going to be real happy, and I might just find him in his own turf, with his friends around him. I explained that to her. She walked me to the door.

"If you find him like that," she said, touching my arm, "be careful. Don't approach him."

"I'll just tail him and find out where he lives. That's all."

"That's all she wants."

"I'll remember."

I left the house and got into the rental car. Lisa just wanted to confront him. I'd started this thing as a favor for Sam, but the more I thought about Drew deliberately infecting women with a deadly virus, the more I just wanted to smash his face in. How the hell could somebody justify doing that? I just couldn't understand it, and I doubted he could ever explain it to me.

5

There were plenty of bars and restaurants down on the Landing, as Lisa had said, but I'd already been to three places where Ted Drew used to hang out, and they were all of a type. They all served food, but none of them could have been called restaurants. With that in mind I walked along and stopped at bar and grill type places, had one beer and looked around. A couple of them catered to a younger crowd, so after a single beer I rejected them. Both Lisa and Kitty were in their thirties, so I figured that was the kind of girl Drew would go for.

I didn't ask questions this time, either. If he was currently hanging out in any of these places I didn't want to scare him off. If he was the barhopping type—which he seemed to be— then if I didn't spot him this night, I would the next, or the one after that. He wouldn't be able to stay away.

I worked the Landing for three days and nights until the bars closed, staying away from Lisa and Sam until dinner. I had made up a list of the places I thought Ted Drew might show and I had a beer in one, then moved to the next one, and so on. On Friday, I caught a break, which is usually the way my job finally gets done.

I was in a place called The Big Muddy, sitting at the bar nursing a beer. When the beer was done I was going to move on to the next place on my list. A woman in her early thirties with long brown hair came up to the bar and stood about five stools from me. She was wearing a light blue shirt and dark blue jeans. She stood there and waited for the bartender to notice her.

"Has Ted been around?" she asked, and my ears perked up.

"Not yet," the bartender said.

"Come on, Maury, he's not home he must be—"

"He ain't been in, Lynn, I swear."

"Is he coming in?"

The bartender, a beefy man in his forties, just shrugged.

"He's hiding from me—"

"He's not hiding, Lynn. Why don't you just give up?"

"I don't want to, Maury. Do you think he's at the Rock?"

"I don't know. You could try."

The Rock was another bar that was on my list. When she left I decided to follow her.

Walking along behind her I couldn't help wondering if she'd slept with Drew yet, if she'd been infected. From her conversation with the bartender, it sounded like she wanted to find Drew, but he didn't want any part of her. Maybe there was something I could do before anything happened.

She went into the Rock and I stepped in behind her, remaining just inside the door. She went up to the bartender and talked to him, and I saw him shake his head and shrug. She slammed her hand down on the bar once and he spread his hands in a helpless gesture. As she turned to leave, a patron sitting at the bar said something to her and she spoke sharply, cutting him down, and started past him. He reached out and grabbed her arm and I saw her wince.

The man was in his late thirties and big, but he was carrying some extra weight around his middle that would slow him down. This looked like my chance to meet Lynn.

I moved toward the bar and stopped just on the other side of the man.

". . . think you're too good. You ain't even that good-looking."

"Then let go of my arm." Lynn's voice sounded calm, like she'd dealt with this kind of thing before. Up-close I could see that the man was wrong, though. She was kind of cute, and I'd walked along behind her from the Muddy and knew she filled her jeans out okay. He was just smarting from being brushed off.

The bartender came over to me and I said, "Busch, in a bottle."

Lynn was trying to soothe the man's wounded ego now, telling him she was sorry but she just didn't have time.

"It didn't sound to me like your man was gonna be around, so why not have a drink with me?"

"Look, I'm trying to be nice—"

"No, you ain't," the man said, cutting her off. "That's the problem."

The bartender brought my beer, cast a look at Lynn and the man, and walked to the other end of the bar.

I picked up my beer in my left hand and with my right I tapped the guy on the shoulder.

"Huh?" He turned his head to look over his shoulder at me. With my rigid index finger I poked him in the eye.

"Ow, Jesus!" He released Lynn and put both hands up to his face. I pushed my beer in front of him and looked at Lynn.

"Come on," I said.

She looked unsure, but I took her hand and led her outside.

"T-thanks."

"That's okay. With that kind of guy you just have to give them something else to think about."

She examined my face, then smiled and said, "That makes sense."

"I heard you asking for Ted. Would that be Ted Drew?"

"Do you know Ted?"

"No, but I'm looking for him, too."

Now she looked suspicious.

"Oh, yeah? Why?"

"Are you his girl?"

She bit her lips a moment, then said, "I thought I was."

"And you'd still like to be?"

She stared at me a moment, then nodded.

"Let's go someplace and talk."

"I don't know—"

"There something very important you should know about Ted."

"I thought you said you didn't know him?"

"I don't," I said, "but I know something about him."

"What?"

"Let's get a drink, Lynn."

I figured she was going to need one.

6

There was a McDonald's on the Landing so we went there to talk instead of a bar. We both got coffee and found a table.

"What do you want to tell me about Ted?" she asked.

"First, can you tell me where he lives now?"

"What for?"

"I want to find him, Lynn."

"Are you a cop?"

"Is Ted afraid of the cops?"

"No, why should he be?"

"Why are you asking me if I'm a cop?"

"You look like a cop."

I looked at her and smiled. "How many cops do you know?"

"None."

"Lynn, how . . . close are you and Ted Drew?"

"We're . . . tight."

"That explains why you can't find him."

"We had a fight. It's nothing serious."

"But he's avoiding you."

"So what? He . . . he loves me. I know he does."

"Lynn . . ." I leaned forward. "Have you slept with him?"

"Sure I have."

She said it too fast. I sat back in my chair.

"Lynn, I'm a private detective. I know two girls who have been infected with AIDS by Ted Drew."

Her eyes went wide. "That can't be true."

I took the picture Lisa gave me from my pocket. "Is this Ted?"

She looked at the picture and nodded.

"Then it's true. He's given two women AIDS that I know of. There could be many more. I'll ask you again. Have you had sex with him?"

She looked drugged.

"No." Her tone was listless. "I wanted to, but he didn't want no part of me."

"You're a lucky girl, then."

She rubbed both hands over her face, then looked at me.

"Is it true?"

"Yes, it's true."

"Jesus. I never thought I'd feel so glad a guy dumped me. But . . . he doesn't look sick . . . except he wasn't feeling too good the last time I saw him. He said he had a . . . a bug, or something."

He had a bug, all right.

"I've got to find him, Lynn. Will you help me?"

"I can give you his address. He wasn't home when I banged on his door."

"When was that?"

"All week."

"Give me the address and I'll check it out."

I took a small pad out of my pocket and she wrote his address on it, then told me how to get there.

"Count yourself lucky, Lynn. Be more careful in the future who you pick."

She laughed ironically and said, "You know the first day I went to his place I thought he was cheating on me. I mean, I felt like he was."

"Why?"

"I saw two women coming from his apartment."

"Coming out of his apartment?"

"No, just from that direction. I banged on his door and when there was no answer I figured I was wrong. Besides, there looked like something was wrong with one of them."

"Like what?"

"She was holding her arm stiff, and the other woman was supporting her."

"What'd they look like?"

"Well . . . they looked like me, sort of. Long dark hair, slender, about my age. I thought maybe Ted liked that type, you know? He wasn't home, though, so they weren't coming from his place. I guess I ought to thank you, mister. You probably saved my life."

"Maybe. From now on, though, make sure you save your own, all right?"

She nodded and I left, feeling like a commercial for safe sex.

I followed her instructions to an apartment complex on

Gravois and Grand. When I got to Drew's apartment there was no bell, just a knocker. I used it a couple of times, then peered in the window next to the door. I saw furniture, but if he rented furnished apartments that explained that. There was other stuff around, though. Magazines, newspaper, some fast-food wrappers on a coffee table. It looked to me like someone still lived there.

The apartment was one of six in this building, and it was on the first floor. I walked around to the back and saw that there were patios, and sliding-glass doors. The gate was on a latch and easy to open. When I got to the sliding-glass door I found it locked. I couldn't see any way to get in short of breaking the glass, and that wasn't my place to do. I peered into the room. It was a kitchen, with a cheap aluminum table and two metal folding chairs. I was about to give up when I spotted something else. I moved all the way to my right to give myself a better angle and saw what it was. Sticking out from behind the kitchen counter was a shoe—with a foot attached.

7

Ted Drew was dead. He'd been stabbed in his kitchen. The place was a mess behind the counter, which I was unable to see from outside the door. There were pots and pans and glass all over the floor, and a lot of blood.

I told the police the whole story. There was no reason not to. I also told them I was doing a favor for a friend, not working for a fee. After all, I wasn't licensed in the state of Missouri. They took my statement, my name, address, and phone number. After that they let me go. I drove directly back to Lisa's house.

★ ★ ★ ★ ★

"How was he killed?" Lisa asked.

"He was stabbed. Well, actually it looked as if he was stabbed during a fight."

"So then he didn't . . ."

"No, he didn't die of the disease."

"That's too bad. I'll call Kitty and tell her."

She was cold, real cold, but who could blame her. She just wanted him to die of the same disease she knew she was going to die of.

"I guess there's not much more to say, Nick. Thanks for trying to help."

She made it sound like I had failed. Hell, she wanted me to find him and I did. It wasn't my fault she and Kitty had killed him.

"Sam, it's time to leave."

"But—"

"I really think it's time to leave. We can change our tickets at the airport." We'd been scheduled to leave in two more days, but I didn't want to stay any longer.

It took Sam fifteen minutes to pack. She and Lisa embraced, but over Sam's shoulder Lisa's eyes met mine, and I think she saw that I knew.

"Stay in touch, please," Sam said.

Lisa promised she would, but it was a promise she never kept. Ultimately, she locked herself away from her family and friends and just waited to die—or go to jail.

On the way to the airport I explained it to Sam.

"I don't believe it," she said. "How could you think that Lisa and Kitty killed him?"

"They're members of the same club, remember?"

"Nick—"

"It all fits, Sam. Lynn saw two women walking away from

159

Drew's building last Monday. According to the M.E., Drew would have been dead about then. That's why he didn't answer the door when Lynn knocked."

"So how does—"

"Let me finish. She said one of the women was supporting the other, and one was holding her arm. I don't know who was supporting who, but Kitty has a bandage on her hand. I think she got cut during the fight."

"And Lisa?"

"She's limping. There was broken glass on the floor. I think that's what she got in her foot, not a nail."

"But why would she kill him, and then ask me to help?"

"Did she ask you for help? For my help?"

"Well . . . no, now that I think of it. I offered to have you help her, but that was only when she said she wished she could find him."

"She knew he was dead when she said that, Sam. She just thought that was what she was supposed to say. When you offered to have me find him, she must have thought it would sound suspicious if she refused. Besides, it'll make a good argument when they arrest her. She'll ask the cops why she would have me searching for him if she killed him."

Sam folded her arms across her breasts.

"I don't believe it."

"Well, I do."

We drove in silence for a while and then she asked, "What are you going to do?"

"Nothing."

"Nothing? You think they committed murder and you're not going to say anything to the police?"

"No."

"Why not?"

"Because if I figured it out the cops will, too, eventually.

Let Lisa and Kitty think they got away with it a little longer."

"Why would you do that?"

"Because they don't have anything else. Besides, I don't think they went there to kill him. I think they went there to confront him, and things got out of hand. Maybe he ridiculed them and there was a fight, and the two of them were able to kill him. He was only stabbed once, so it could have been an accident. If they'd gone there to kill him I think they would have both stabbed him several times before stopping."

We drove a little more in silence before Sam spoke again.

"I still can't believe it."

At least she didn't say she "didn't" believe it.

"Forget it, Sam. Let's just get back to Brooklyn."

Like a Stranger

1

Strangers come into your life every day. Some stay strangers, some become friends, some hover in that neverland between those two as "acquaintances." How often, though, do strangers come into your life claiming that they're not strangers, but old friends?

But I should start at the beginning, shouldn't I?

I was only home a few moments when there was a knock on my door. It had become a familiar knock over the past few years so I knew even before opening it that I'd find Samantha Karson—aka Kit Karson when she was writing her romance novels—standing in the hall.

"It's here," she said immediately. "I got copies in the mail today."

"What's here?"

"The book, you dope," she said, moving past me into my apartment.

I'd been living at the Sackett Street address for about six years at this point, and for about half that time Sam had been my neighbor. During all that time she had been writing her romances, but lamenting about the fact that what she really wanted to write was mystery novels.

"Oh," I said, "that book."

"Here," she said, and held it out to me.

It was a hardcover novel, where her dozen or so romances had been paperback originals. The title, *TOO BLONDE TO BE DUMB*, was something we had gone round and round about, and I had been surprised when her publisher agreed with her that it was a good one. Her character, a private investigator named Nick Dellesandro—nee Bernadette Nicole Dellesandro—was a thinly disguised female version of me.

"Open it to the dedication page."

"Which one is that?"

She looked exasperated, reached over and flipped a couple of pages, then stopped.

It read: *To my good friend Nick, without whom Nicole never would have been born.*

"I'm touched," I said, then aware that it might have sounded less than sincere added, "I'm really touched, Sam. Thank you."

"Well, you really helped me a lot, Nick."

I closed the book and looked at the cover. It was a reproduction of a photograph of what the cover artist thought was a typical Brooklyn street, since the series was set in Brooklyn.

"Is this . . ." I started to ask.

"Your copy," she said. "Keep it."

"You have to sign it," I said.

She accepted it back, looked around for a pen—I had to go into my office to get one for her—and then took a moment to think before signing it and handing it back.

"Don't look at it until I leave," she said, hurriedly heading for the door.

When she got to the door she opened it, then turned quickly and said, "Oh, a friend of yours was here."

"Was where?"

"Here," she said. "I mean, he knocked on my door after knocking on yours."

"Did you get a name?"

"Yes," she said, "his name was Dave Hollins."

"Dave Hollins?" I repeated, frowning. "I don't know any Dave Hollins."

"He said you and he were buddies in high school," she said. "In fact, he said 'best buddies.' "

My frown deepened.

"I don't remember any Dave Hollins from high school. Did he say what he wanted?"

"No, he didn't," she said. "God, Nick, if I had a best buddy in high school I'd sure remember their name. Shame on you."

"No," I said, "it's not that I don't remember his name. I never knew a Dave Hollins."

"Well," she said, "he said he'd get back to you. Are you going to read the book tonight?"

She wouldn't let me read it while she was writing it all those months, and now that it was out she wanted me to read it in one night.

"I'll start it tonight, Sam," I said. "I don't know when I'll finish it."

"Well, all right," she said, "but I want to know what you think . . . honestly."

"I'll tell you," I said, "honestly. By the way."

"Yeah?"

I held the book up and said, "Congratulations. How about I buy you dinner to celebrate?"

"Your treat?"

"I said I'd buy, didn't I?"

"My choice?"

"You're on," she said. "I'll be ready at six."

"I'll knock on your door."

She left, closing the door behind her, and I opened the

book to see what she had written inside. She'd used the very first page of the book, which was blank. She had written:

> *To my best friend, Nick*
> *Thanks for believing in me,*
> *for always being there for me. I love you.*
> *Sam*

Well, I guess I loved her too, but as a friend, you know? And we were friends, the best of friends, and she had been there for me even more, I thought, than I had for her.

I put the book down, feeling a tightness inside, feeling glad that Sam was my friend, and then wondering who this other fella was who was claiming to be my friend?

That was the first time I heard of Dave Hollins.

It was far from the last.

2

Over the course of the next few days I heard about Dave Hollins, my "buddy," two more times. Once from my father, who said he called his house looking for me.

"He said he was a friend of yours, Nicky."

"So you gave him my address?"

"Why shouldn't I give your address to an old friend?" my father asked.

"It's okay, Pop," I said, "don't worry about it."

The next day I heard from my brother, Father Vinnie.

"A friend of yours dropped by the church, Nicky."

"Who, Vinnie?"

"Dave Hollins, from high school."

"Vinnie, do you remember a Dave Hollins from high

school?" My brother had been a year ahead of me.

"No," Vinnie said, "and he didn't look familiar, either, Nick. You don't know him?"

"No."

"What's going on?"

"I don't know," I said, "but I'm going to find out."

I looked up Dave Hollins in the phone book but there was no listing. I called a few friends from high school, but no one had ever heard of him. In between doing these things I tried reading Sam's book. I say I tried because it just wasn't something I'd normally read. She'd written what she called a "hard-boiled" private eye novel, but it all seemed pretty silly to me. I couldn't tell her that, though. Hey, some editor had bought the book and published it, so it must have had some merit, right? I'd always been able to see the talent in Sam's writing, but I bet if she went in a different direction she could write something really special.

Hey, what did I know? Maybe mystery fans would love it. For her sake I hoped so. Now all I had to do was think of something diplomatic to say to her that wouldn't convey how I really felt.

I left Sam's book half read and continued my search for Dave Hollins.

I went to my old high school in the Bensonhurst section of Brooklyn to look up Dave Hollins. I had just about decided that he didn't exist when I found him in the school records. I knew the girl who worked in the office because we *had* gone to school together, and she'd ended up working there. She was an Irish girl named Shannon, and she let me look through the records.

"I never heard of him, Nick," she said, when I pulled his records.

"Well, here he is." I dropped the file on her desk and took a look through it. He appeared to have been an average student, maybe a little below, and didn't appear to have played on any teams. I'd played baseball, football and basketball, and I knew he hadn't been on any of those teams. According to his file, he hadn't even been in the chess club.

"Shannon, can you pull the yearbook?"

"Which one?"

I checked the date that he had graduated.

"Ours," I said, surprised. "He graduated with us."

"I'll get the book."

She pulled it from a set of shelves and opened it on her desk. We leafed through it together. There was only one photo of Dave Hollins and it didn't say anything underneath it. Dave Hollins had apparently had the most unremarkable four years of high school of any student I'd ever known.

"God," Shannon said, "It looks like even the geeks had nothing to do with him. Why's he going around telling everyone that you and he were friends?"

"I don't know. Maybe I should ask him."

"How?"

"I'll check the last address you have for him. Maybe he still has family there."

She got a 3x5 index card and wrote the address down for me. Hollins had lived three blocks from where we lived, where my dad still lived.

"Thanks, Shannon. I owe you. How about lunch?"

"Dinner."

"All right, dinner. I'll call you."

"If it's okay with you, Nicky, I won't hold my breath."

3

I went to the address on Dave Hollins' file and found a house much like the one I had grown up in. It was brick, a single story, attached on one side with a driveway on the other. As far as I knew I had never been there before in my life.

I went to the door, hoping that at least his mother or some family member still lived there. I was quite surprised when a man about my age opened the door in response to the doorbell.

He was balding prematurely, and was overweight, but there was enough resemblance to the photo in the yearbook for me to know that this was Dave Hollins.

I opened my mouth to speak but before I could say a word his face split into a big grin and he grabbed me, yelling, "Nicky-D!"

He hugged me tightly in a bearhug, pinning my arms to my side. He was not that strong and while I could have broken the hold I suffered the embrace until he released me and stepped back.

"Goddamn it's good to see you, man." He was speaking very quickly. "Come on in. How'd you find me? I've been trying to find you for days. I talked to your father, and your brother—hey, Vinnie's a priest now, huh? That's great! Come on in, follow me . . ."

He kept talking a mile a minute as I followed him into the house, waiting until I could get a word in. I closed the door behind me and followed him to a musty smelling but neat living room. The house smelled as if he never opened a window.

". . . place looks the same, hasn't changed much since my mom died last year."

"I'm . . . sorry—" I said, but that was all I was able to get out.

"Ah, it's okay," he said, cutting me off, "she was old, ya know? Hey, you want a brew?"

"Uh, no—"

"Some coffee? I can make some instant."

"No, thanks. Listen. Dave—"

"Come on, sit down," Hollins said. "We've got to catch up on old times, huh?"

"Well, uh, actually, no, we don't."

"What?" He looked puzzled.

"What I mean is, uh . . ." I tried to think of a delicate way to put it. "As far as I know, uh, Dave, we don't have any old times to catch up on."

"What are you talkin' about, Nick?"

"Dave—uh, Mr. Hollins, what I'm saying is . . ." I finally decided to just go ahead and blurt it out. "I don't know you."

"Huh?"

"I don't know any other way to put it," I said, gently. "I don't know who you are."

He stared at me for a few moments with the look of a hurt puppy on his face, then smiled, as if he thought I was kidding.

"Aw, c'mon! You're pullin' my leg, right?"

"I'm not kidding."

He stared at me.

"You're not?"

I shook my head.

He remained silent for a few moments, then slid his hands into his pockets and said, "Well, I guess I look more than a little foolish, huh? I thought we were friends, Nicky."

I made a helpless gesture with my hands and said, "If we were and I don't remember, Dave, I'm really sorry, but to tell you the truth, I checked with some of the other people I know from school, and nobody remembers you."

"Your brother," he said. "I talked to Vinnie the other day—"

"He doesn't remember you. I'm sorry."

He stared at me, his expression unreadable, now, maybe a cross between disappointment and disbelief.

"You really don't remember?"

I shook my head.

"I'm sorry," I said again, "you're a stranger to me," and then left the house.

What else could I do? I wasn't going to pretend I knew the guy.

What else could I have done?

4

I thought that would be the end of things with Dave Hollins, but I was wrong.

Two days later Sam was in my apartment wanting to know if I'd finished her book, yet.

"Almost."

"How do you like it?"

"I don't want to say anything until I'm finished."

"You hate it."

I frowned at her.

"I don't hate it," I said, "there are just one or two things . . ."

"Like what?"

"Well . . . you have your Nick get into fights—"

"Women don't get into fights?"

"That's not it," I said. "Here, look, page . . ." I grabbed the book. ". . . one twenty-eight. She knees this guy in the face hard enough to break his jaw."

"And that can't happen?"

"Sure, it can happen . . . but afterwards, she doesn't even limp."

"So you're saying it's not realistic?"

"I guess that's what I'm saying . . . but like I said, I'm not done. I don't want to talk about it anymore."

"All right, all right, I'll wait until you're finished."

She walked to the window and looked out.

"Who are you looking for?" I asked.

"The mailman. I'm waiting for a check from my agent. Hey!"

"What?"

"That's your friend, down there."

"What friend?"

"You know, that Hollins guy."

"I already told you he's not my friend."

"Well then, why's he down there looking up at your window?"

I crossed the room to stand next to her and look down. Sure enough, Dave Hollins was on the street, hands in his pockets, looking up at my window. The look on his broad face was not a pleasant one.

"Hey, Nick. You got your very own stalker?"

"I'm not going to stand for this," I said, and rushed from my apartment. By the time I got down the two flights of steps, though, he was gone. I looked both ways, but he was nowhere in sight.

The mailman was, though.

"You better get in there," I said to him. "You got a desperate woman waiting for you."

"I try to satisfy them all," he said, "but it can't be done."

I stayed on the street until the mailman came back out,

then went inside. Sam was at her mailbox and I stuck my key in mine.

"Yes, it's here!" she said, triumphantly. I had a mailbox full of bills, and was somewhat less enthusiastic than she was.

"Did you talk to him?" she asked.

"He was gone when I got down there."

"What's his problem?"

"As far as I can tell he never had any friends in high school," I said. "Maybe he still doesn't."

"So he picked you?"

"Maybe," I said, "but as soon as I get a hold of him he's going to *un*pick me."

5

I went to Hollins' house again but he wasn't there. When I got back home he was nowhere to be seen. There were a couple of messages on my machine so I pressed the button to play them back.

"Nick, it's-a you father. That guy came around again yesterday. He wasn't a-so friendly, this time. He said some-a bad things about you, like you forget-a you friends. Whatsa his problem, Nicky, huh? Call me."

Pop was born in Italy and when he was upset his accent came back. I'd ring Hollins' neck for getting him worried.

The second message surprised me. It was from Hollins,

"Hey, Nick, old friend? I'm gonna give you a chance to make it up to me for not remembering me. I got somebody with me who apparently you're real friendly with. She's a real pretty blonde with nice big tits. The rest of this message is on her machine, ol' buddy."

That sonofabitch, he had Sam . . . or did he?

I rushed from my apartment to her door, which was ajar. Bad sign. I went inside and there was one message flashing on her machine. I pressed the Play button.

"Nick? I'm sorry, he knocked on my door and—" Sam's voice was cut off and Hollins came on. "Sorry, that's all you get to hear, ol' pal. Want more? Meet us on the roof . . . now!"

On the roof? *My* roof? What the hell was he doing?

I left Sam's apartment and ran up the steps to the roof. Sure enough when I got outside he and Sam were there, and the sonofabitch was smiling. They were standing too close to the edge to suit me.

"I love technology," he said, showing me a cellular phone in one hand. "Your girlfriend was kind enough to give me her number, so I could convince you to join us."

Sam was standing just to his left, her posture stiff.

"Sam, come over here by me."

"I can't, Nick."

"Why not?"

"He's got a gun."

He brought his other hand out from behind his back now and she was right, he was holding a gun. It was a flat automatic, small but deadly. He spread his hands now, phone in one and the gun in the other.

"Okay, Hollins, what's it going to be? What do you want?"

"What do I want?" Hollins asked. "What did I ever want from any of you but a little friendship?"

"Come on," I said, "this is some grievance from high school, is that it? We're a long way from high school, Hollins."

"Dave," he said, "my name's Dave. I can't believe you still don't remember me."

"What's she got to do with this, Dave?" I asked. "Let her go."

174

"No." He dropped the phone to the ground and used his free hand to grab Sam's arm. He looked like a doughboy standing next to her, but a dangerous and maybe deranged one.

"You don't remember all the times in high school you talked to me, do you?" he demanded.

"I'm sorry, man . . . I don't."

"After a football game or a baseball game, after we won you'd come off the field and yell 'Come on, let's party.' You'd be looking right at me when you said it!"

I couldn't believe what I was hearing. Whenever we won a game I yelled that to the crowd, never specifically to anyone. Did he really think I'd been talking to him? Was that what he based this whole fantasy friendship on?

"Dave, come on," I said, "I yelled that to everyone."

"To me!" he shouted. "You looked right at me. 'Come on,' you said, 'let's party.' "

Sam was watching me, her eyes wide with fright. She didn't scare easy, but this guy was off his rocker, and that frightened her.

It scared me, too.

"Look, Dave," I said, soothingly, "why don't you put the gun down. Let's go down to my place and talk about old times."

"Old times?" he asked. "Now you want me to believe you remember old times?"

"Maybe you can make me remember them, Dave. You know, as a matter of fact, I think I do remember you, now. You've put on a little weight, man. You were kind of thin in school, weren't you?"

He frowned at me, I guess wondering if I was speaking from memory or not.

"And your hairline, it used to be right here, didn't it?" I ran my forefinger along my forehead, where his hairline had

175

been in his yearbook photo.

"Yeah, that's right," he said, "it was. I started losing it last year, when my mom died. She . . . she was the only family, the only friend I had. When she died I had nobody."

"You should have called me when she died, man," I said, "I could have helped you out."

"I called," he said, "I called a lot of guys from high school. It took me this long to get to you."

"Jesus, Dave," I said, "you should have called me first. We were buddies, remember?"

Now he was confused. He maintained his hold on Sam's arm, wiped his mouth with the back of his other hand, bringing the gun up in front of his face.

"What are you doing with the gun, Dave?"

"You wanna laugh?" he asked. "I bought it to kill myself with."

"There's no need for that."

"Why not? You said yourself, Nick, nobody remembers me."

"So what, Dave?" I said. "That was high school, a long time ago. Who cares about those people? You're all grown up now, make yourself some new friends."

"That's easy to say. I—I was never able to make friends, not then, and not now."

"Dave, look at Sam. Look at her!"

He turned his head and did as I said.

"See how frightened she is? How much you're scaring her? That's not the way to make friends."

"I haven't hurt her, have I? Ask her. Have I hurt you, Miss?"

"N-no . . ."

"See?"

"That's good, Dave, but it's time to go in now."

"I don't want to."

"Then let Sam go in," I said. "I'll stay out here with you and we can talk."

He looked uncertain.

"Do you promise?"

"I promise," I said. "Just let her go. She's got nothing to do with this."

"You care about her, don't you?"

"Yes, I do," I said. "I care about her a lot."

"See? That's all I've ever wanted, somebody to care about what happens to me."

"I care, Dave."

"Really?"

"I do."

Hollins hesitated a few moments, then suddenly wrapped his arm around Sam and pulled her close to him. My stomach lurched when he pressed the gun to her neck.

"Don't do that, Dave!"

"Why not?"

"What's it going to solve?"

"Maybe you'll feel bad," he said. "Maybe you'll wish you'd been nicer to me. Maybe I'll shoot her, and then myself."

"And then what? Maybe I'll just forget about you."

"Huh?" He looked confused.

"When you're gone people forget about you. Is that what you want?"

"N-no."

"And what about your mother?"

"What about her?"

"If you kill yourself, who's going to remember her? You said she was all you had, so I guess you were all she had, right?"

"R-right."

"Then you don't want her to be forgotten, do you?"

"N-no, I don't."

"Well, that's what'll happen. If you die, nobody will remember either one of you."

Dave Hollins stood with the gun pressed to Sam's neck and thought it over.

"Put the gun down, Dave. We'll go inside and order a pizza. What do you say?"

Again he hesitated, giving it some thought. He waited so long I thought I had him, but then the expression on his face changed and I knew I'd lost him again.

"No! You're lying." He backed up a few steps, bringing himself and Sam closer to the edge of the roof.

"Dave, look at what you're doing. Look at this scene, man. Don't you recognize it?"

"What are you talking about?"

"Don't you ever watch television? Whenever the bad guy ends up on the roof he goes over the edge—and that's going to hurt, Dave."

He frowned.

"Look how close you are to the edge already."

It was my last chance, and I took it. He turned his head to look at the edge of the roof and I charged him. He was taking a couple of steps away from the edge when he heard me. I knew when I was several feet from him that I didn't have enough time.

That's when Sam moved. She simply went limp and Hollins, not being especially strong, couldn't hold her. I dove and hit him in the midsection as he was trying to bring the gun around. We both staggered back towards the edge of the roof, and for a moment I thought we were going to rewrite the script. I thought the bad guy *and* the good guy were going to go over, but his knees went out from beneath him and we tumbled to the roof. As we hit the gun was jarred from his hand and went skidding away. I rolled away from him towards the gun, regained my feet before him and snatched it up.

As I turned to point it at him he was on his hands and knees, trying to get up, when Sam charged him and smashed him in the face with her knee. He cried out and fell over, unconscious, bleeding profusely from the broken nose.

Sam yelled in pain and went down, holding her knee.

"Sonofabitch!" I didn't know if she meant Hollins, or if she was just cursing from the pain.

I walked to her and crouched next to her.

"Are you all right?"

"I think I broke my knee, Nick."

I knew her knee wasn't broken, just bruised, so I smiled at her, put my arms around her and said, "Put that in your next book."

The Old Dons

1

Don Dominick Barracondi was an old Don.

In his case "old" had two meanings. First, he was in his sixties, past his prime. And second, once the Godfather of Brooklyn he had been "retired" for some time, supposedly "out of it." Having been my father's best friend for years, I inherited him as my real godfather, so when he called and asked me to come see him, I couldn't refuse.

He started by telling me he had an illegitimate daughter, which I never knew. He had been sending her mother money until the girl turned eighteen, but had no contact with her personally. Now she was twenty-five and had gotten herself in trouble—if you call murder "trouble."

The Don had been contacted by a blackmailer, who said Carol had been involved in a murder in Atlantic City when she and her rock band, "Bad News," played there. They had since moved on, but if the Don didn't pay within four days, the blackmailer was going to turn certain "evidence" over to the cops. "Carol Dee," as she was calling herself—DiConstanzo had been her mother's name—would then be arrested for murder.

The Don offered me money to go to Atlantic City and check this story out. I refused—the money, that is. I said I would do it for expenses, as a favor. Don Dominick thought that was smart of me, putting him in my debt.

I hadn't thought of it that way, but I liked the idea.

Hal Devlin was a detective in the 69th Precinct, who had arrested my brother, Father Vinnie, for murder a couple of years ago. I cleared my brother, but ended up in the same poker game with Devlin. It was for that reason I knew he went to Atlantic City often.

That was how I ended up making the drive with Detective Hal Devlin.

The only thing I knew about Atlantic City I learned from a monopoly board. I saw Utah Avenue and Pacific Avenue and eventually we ended up by the Boardwalk. I couldn't tell whether we had ever passed Go.

After we exited the Atlantic City Expressway I noticed we were heading *away* from the Boardwalk.

"There are two hotel/casinos on the bay side," Devlin told me, "Harrah's Marina and ours, the King's Tower."

The King's Tower wasn't a tower, but an ultra modern high rise with a rainbow on its roof. The lobby reception area was on the third floor, as was the casino. As we approached the reception desk I stared up at a six-story, glass-encased atrium. The lobby itself was largely marble and brass. When we reached the front desk Devlin asked for Tony Ciccio, head of security.

We didn't have long to wait before a wiry, dapper-looking man in an expensively cut suit came through a door behind the desk.

"Hello, Tony," Devlin said, shaking the man's hand vigorously. "This is my friend, Nick Delvecchio."

"Mr. Delvecchio," Ciccio said, shaking my hand. Ciccio had slicked black hair and appeared to be in his early forties. He probably stood no more than five-seven. We shook hands and he asked if I was a gambler.

"Not really," I said. "I'm here on business."

"Business?" He frowned and looked at Devlin.

"Delvecchio is a New York P.I.," Hal said. "He's here on a case, Tony. I'm helping him out. That means I'll want you to help me out."

Ciccio said, "I see."

"Can you come up to our suite?"

"I can," Ciccio said, "if you give me about an hour."

"Good," Devlin said, "now can you get us a suite?"

Ciccio smiled then, a genuinely friendly smile and said, "Wait here."

"Impressive, huh?" Devlin said, spreading his arms. "Two bedrooms, a fully stocked bar—you want a drink?" Devlin went around behind the marble-topped counter.

"Not for me, thanks. Tell me about Ciccio."

Devlin told me Ciccio was an ex-A.C. cop who left the job when he got the offer to head security at the hotel.

"How did you meet?"

"He came to New York one time to pick up a prisoner and I showed him the sights," Devlin said. "He'd come back and we'd do it up again. When he got this job he said I was comped any time I showed up."

"Nice of him."

"He's good people, Delvecchio," Devlin said. "He's still got plenty of A.C. police contacts."

"Well," I said, "we've got almost an hour. I think I'll take a shower."

"Each bedroom has its own bathroom. Take your pick."

I went into one bedroom, looked up at the huge ceiling, then stared at the mile long bed. Devlin may have liked all the glitter, but not me. I was starting to miss my apartment in Brooklyn.

★ ★ ★ ★ ★

Tony Ciccio showed up at our suite about an hour later.

"Tony, Delvecchio here needs to get a look at homicide cases for . . ." I supplied him with the dates.

"What's this about?" Ciccio asked.

"I have a client who may be involved in a murder here in Atlantic City," I said.

"What makes you think that?"

"Ah . . ." I said, and Devlin jumped in to save me.

"This is all kind of confidential, Tony. Do you have a friend in homicide?"

"Sure," Ciccio said, "but whether or not he helps is another thing."

"How will he react when I flash my tin?"

"If it was for you," Ciccio said, "on official business, I'm sure he'd cooperate, but for a P.I.—"

"Well, just get us the intro, Tony."

"I'll talk to him," Ciccio said.

"Today?" Devlin asked.

Ciccio laughed and said, "Yeah, sure, Hal, today. Where will you guys be?"

"Where else?" Devlin asked. "In the casino."

"I'll be in touch."

I play poker, and I've been known to bet on a horse, but that's as far as my gambling goes. When we walked into the casino I was overwhelmed. The lights, the noise, the loud music being piped in. Devlin rubbed his hands together with unrestrained glee.

"I love this, Nick," he said. "I fuckin' love this."

"What do you play, Hal?"

"Blackjack."

To Devlin, blackjack was the only game worth playing.

He led me to a table with a little sign on it that read: $10 to

$200. It was early, and half the chairs were empty.

"Two hundred," Devlin said. He tossed the dealer bills, and received the equal amount in chips.

I watched Devlin for an hour. He was very intense. He also seemed to be very good. By the end of the hour he was up five hundred dollars.

Bored, I was trying to decide whether to buy in when I felt someone tap me on the shoulder. I turned around, then looked down and saw Tony Ciccio. He had a genial smile on his face.

"My man's here. Where's Hal?"

"Playing blackjack, but we don't have to bother him."

"Yes, we do," Ciccio said. "We'll need his shield."

We walked over to the blackjack table.

"Hal," Ciccio said, putting his hand on Devlin's shoulder the same way he'd done to me. "I've got someone you want to meet."

Devlin looked down at his chips.

"I could use a break, anyway."

He picked up his chips and got up from the table. We started walking with Ciccio.

As soon as we entered Ciccio's office I knew it was going to cost me money. It was in the attitude and demeanor of the man sitting behind the desk.

He was in his mid-forties, dressed at least ten years too young. His shirt was open at the collar, a gold chain hung around his neck. His thinning, black hair was combed across his head to try and hide the fact he was balding. The room reeked of cologne, and he had a couple of rings on each hand. He had his Gucci shoes up on Ciccio's desk.

"This is Detective Alan Royale," Ciccio said. "Alan, meet Detective Hal Devlin of the N.Y.P.D."

"Devlin," Royale said, inclining his head.

"Yeah," Devlin said, "glad to meet you."

Royale looked away from Devlin and stared at me.

"Delvecchio," I said, since no one else did.

"You on the job, babe?" I hate people who call me "pal," "buddy," or "chief"—and "babe" was a particular non-favorite of mine.

"No."

He directed his attention back to Devlin.

"You got your tin, babe?"

Devlin showed it to Royale, who nodded.

"Just bein' careful."

"Have you got yours?" I asked.

He stared at me, then took an alligator wallet from his breast pocket and showed us his shield.

"Thanks," I said.

"I assume this isn't official," Royale said, tucking it away again. "Since we're not exactly going through channels here."

"It's my friend Delvecchio who needs the help."

That interested him, and I knew why. Devlin was a "brother," Royale would have been bound to help him for free. He didn't have that problem with me.

"Why don't you tell me what you need, babe?"

I ran it down for him, saying nothing about the Don.

"What's this group called?" he asked when I finished.

"Bad News."

"Never heard of them. Where'd they play?"

"Convention Hall."

"Couldn't make any of the hotels, huh? I'll have to pull some records that aren't usually for general consumption . . . I mean, you can get police records but there's usually a fee . . ."

I waited to hear a price.

"You know what I mean, babe?"

"I know what you mean, Detective Royale." It was all I could do not to call him "babe."

He got to his feet and walked up to me. "Call me Alan, huh? I mean, we are all friends here, right?"

He looked at Devlin, who grinned at him half-heartedly. Royale had his hand out, so I shook it.

"I'll bring the records here?" he asked.

"As long as you're comfortable with that," I said.

"You know what you'll get will be Xerox copies. Xerox paper being as expensive as it is . . ."

"I understand," I said. "Uh, also, I'm up against a ticking clock."

"No problemo." I could hear the cash register in his head. "I'll have it here tomorrow afternoon."

"Thanks."

"This is good," Royale said, grinning happily at everyone. "It's good, we all understand each other. Tony? I'll be seein' you, babe, huh?" He slapped Ciccio on the shoulder and left.

"That kind of cop . . ." Devlin said, shaking his head.

"He wasn't always like that," Ciccio said.

"What happened?" Devlin asked.

"Hal," Ciccio said. "I know New York is the big ride, but here we get to see high rollers with wads and fancy cars and high-priced hookers on their arms. Sometimes a leaf or two falls off one of those wads . . . you know what I mean?"

"Sure," Devlin said, "I know what you mean . . . babe."

I asked Ciccio, "Did you two work together?"

"Sort of," Ciccio said, moving around behind his desk. "We were partners."

2

As promised, our new friend Alan brought the copies by early the next afternoon. Devlin was in the casino, and I was in our suite waiting when the call came from Tony Ciccio. In the elevator I wondered what Royale would expect to be paid. By the time I reached the door to Ciccio's office I had come up with a figure I thought we could both live with.

I entered and found Ciccio sitting behind his desk and Royale resting a hip on it.

"Afternoon, Delvecchio," Royale said. He held a folder up for me to see and wiggled his eyebrows.

He was dressed similarly to the way he had been yesterday, except everything was a different color. The shirt, something designers probably had a fancy name for, was purple. I've never worn a purple shirt in my life.

"I appreciate this, Alan," I said.

"Uh-huh," he said, still holding the folder aloft in his left hand, leaving his right free.

I approached him, extending my right hand. The bills I had palmed were gone after we shook hands.

"Well, I hope that helps you with your job, babe."

"I'm sure it will."

"If you need more help, let me know." He turned to Ciccio and said, "Tony? See ya, babe."

"Yeah, Alan," Ciccio said. "So long."

I leafed through the material, making sure the copies were all legible, satisfying myself they were.

"Thanks for your help, Tony, I really appreciate it."

"Don't mention it."

I hesitated, wondering if I owed him anything.

"And don't even think about going into your pocket," he said, as if reading my mind.

"Thanks, again."

I headed for the door and he called out, "Hey, Delvecchio?"

"How much did you give him?"

I hesitated a moment, then told him the truth. "Two hundred."

"You could have had him for fifty."

"Now you tell me."

I ordered lunch from room service and started going through the records. Royale had been thorough. During the three days Bad News had been in town there had been three homicides. Royale had included everything, all the detective's follow-up reports, as well as property vouchers.

I took the papers into my bedroom, to a writing desk. I checked each of the homicide reports carefully. Two of them had taken place on or near boardwalk casinos.

The body of a M/W/38—Male, White, 38 years of age—had been found underneath the boardwalk between the Tropicana and Bally's. It was assumed he had come from one of the casinos, and had been rolled for his money. The man had been stabbed. No identification was found.

The detectives checked both hotels, armed with photos of the dead man, and found that he was not registered at either one. Working their way down the boardwalk they finally discovered he was registered at the Sands. His name was Arthur Flourish. A further check of the Sands turned up a couple of dealers who remembered the man as a big loser. Apparently, he had moved onto some other casinos, trying to change his luck. They checked with the employees of the Tropicana and Bally's, but no one remembered him.

The second homicide had taken place in a room at the Showboat, which was way the hell down at the opposite end of the boardwalk from Bally's and the Tropicana. A man named George Grande—a M/W/52—had been shot in his suite. According to the management he was staying there alone, had done some gambling in the casino, and had been a very quiet guest. The detectives could not determine whether he had been a winner or a loser. They assumed he had probably not done enough of either to be noticed.

Room service arrived at that point and I stopped to let the bellboy wheel the cart in. I signed the check and tipped him.

The third homicide had taken place—or at least, the body had been found—in the Farley State Marina, which I could see from my window. Both the marina and my hotel were off Brigantine Blvd. The body of a M/W/26 had been found floating in the marina with no identification. To date, the police still had not identified the body. Checking his prints had come up empty. The man had been killed by a blow to the head with a heavy object, which had not been recovered or identified.

I sat back and opened my second bottle of beer, looking at the Xerox copies I had spread out on the desk. I heard the door to the room open and walked out to see who it was.

"There you are," Hal Devlin said. "Want to get some lunch?"

I held the beer up. "Room service."

"In A.C.?" Devlin said. "Come on, I'll buy you a good meal. I got hot for a while."

"You can buy dinner," I said.

"What are you up to?"

"Checking the reports from our friend Alan Royale."

"Where are they?"

"On the desk."

"Let me take a look."

"I thought you wanted lunch?"

He shrugged and said, "I'll order something from room service."

"In A.C.?" I asked, aghast.

Devlin went through the reports a lot faster than I had, but then I was a little out of practice.

"Doesn't look like much help," he said. "Three men, varying ages, all killed by different methods, two identified, one unidentified—hey, Delvecchio, where was the daughter staying?"

I thought a moment, then said, "I don't know."

"Well, if she was staying here, that would put her in the vicinity of the body in the marina."

"I'll have to check."

"Have you looked at the property vouchers?"

"I was about to when you came in."

There was a knock at the door and Devlin went to admit the bellboy with his lunch. We both went over the property vouchers while he ate and I had another beer. Everything taken from the dead men would be itemized on the vouchers.

From the first homicide—Arthur Flourish—the voucher showed very little: loose change, keys and paper articles.

From George Grande there was quite a bit, as he was killed in his hotel room and the police were forced to voucher everything in the room with him, including his luggage. Where the first voucher had been three lines on one page, Grande's had taken three full sheets.

Again, with the third case—the unidentified floater— there was very little in the way of property.

"Let's put the first and third cases aside and check the vouchers on the second one again," Devlin suggested.

I was grateful for his help, so I was perfectly willing to take his suggestion.

We examined the George Grande vouchers again, and it was Devlin who made the find.

"What's this mean?" he asked.

"What?"

He showed me page 2, item 16.

"Two ticket stubs," I said.

Devlin looked at me and said, "Tickets to what?" and wiggled his eyebrows.

If they were tickets to the Bad News concert, we were in business.

It was late evening when I called Alan Royale's office. I told him what I wanted, he said he'd do it, but assured me it wasn't going to be easy. I told him I'd really appreciate it.

"How much are you gonna pay him for this one?" Devlin asked.

"Maybe he'll throw it in," I said. "After all, he can do it on the phone."

"Sure," Devlin said, "I can see our Detective Royale throwing one in for free, can't you?"

"No," I said, "I can't. Look, how about that dinner you offered to buy?"

"Come on," Devlin said, "we'll eat in the hotel, that way neither one of us will pay." Most of the conversation at dinner revolved around gambling. We were having coffee when the waiter came over to the table.

"Mr. Delvecchio?"

"Yes."

"A phone call for you, sir. You may take it on one of the house phones."

"Thanks." I looked at Devlin. "That's probably our boy."

"Hold onto your wallet."

I walked to a bank of house phones, picked one up and told the operator who I was. She put the call through.

"Delvecchio?" Royale's voice called out jovially.

"Hello, Alan."

"How you doin', babe? How are the tables treatin' you?"

"Just fine," I said. "I appreciate you calling me back."

"I'm sure you do, Delvecchio. This wasn't easy, you know. I had to get somebody to look through everything in the property room, and I mean everything—"

"Believe me, Alan, I really appreciate this."

"Well, sure," Royale said. "Those tickets you wanted to know about? They were for a rock concert."

Trying not to sound too anxious I asked, "What concert was that?"

"Uh, the name of the group was . . ." he snorted before saying, ". . . Bad News, can you believe that?" I wondered if he'd truly forgotten I had mentioned them to him. I couldn't see Royale forgetting anything he'd ever heard, just on the off chance he could turn a profit from it.

"Okay, Alan, thanks. I'll be in touch."

"Sure, babe," Royale said, "I know you will."

When I got back to the table Devlin said, "So."

"Eagle-eye Devlin strikes again," I said. "The ticket stubs were for the Bad News concert."

"Well, there's your connection."

"Just because the man went to the concert doesn't mean Carol Dee met him, or even knew him."

"No," Devlin said, "but you were looking for a connection."

"Yeah, but I can't assume she's involved just from a couple of ticket stubs, can I?"

After dinner Devlin returned to the tables and I went back

to the suite to go through the reports, again.

What I discovered was that I had read them in the wrong order. I decided to take a closer look at the chronological order of the cases.

The actual first homicide was the shooting of George Grande in the Showboat. The second one was the stabbing of Arthur Flourish. Both murders had taken place on the same night. The M.E.'s approximation of the times of death for each indicated both men could have been killed during the same hour.

The body of the unknown man in the marina was found the next morning.

Three homicides in one night?

Even someone who believed in coincidence would find that strange.

I proceeded to go through every scrap of paper Alan Royale had provided for me. Earlier I had keyed on the original report, the detective's supplementary reports, and the property vouchers. This time I read the M.E.'s reports more carefully.

I delved into the envelope again and came up with the fingerprint cards on each of the deceased, and the accompanying reports.

The man from the marina remained unidentified because his prints were not on file anywhere.

George Grande's prints were on file because he had been in the service. Both the prints and a family member who had flown in from his home in North Carolina confirmed his identity.

The report on Arthur Flourish stated that his prints were not on file. The police had also been unable to contact any family at his Pittsburgh, Pennsylvania address.

Grande's body had been found by a maid; Arthur Flourish's body had been discovered by an amorous couple who had apparently intended to have sex under the boardwalk. The body in the marina was found by a security guard.

I'm ashamed to admit it, but up to this point I hadn't really paid much attention to the investigating officer's names on the reports.

Grande's case had been caught by a Detective A. Seitzer.

The Flourish kill had been handled by Detective T. Martinez.

When I looked at the name of the investigating officer on the marina case I don't know why I was surprised. After all, Alan Royale *was* a detective in the homicide squad.

3

Why hadn't Royale told me he'd caught one of those cases? Was he hiding something?

Devlin came back to the room at 3 A.M.

"Found anything?"

"Uh, yeah."

"Formed any theories?"

"Mmm, some farfetched ones, maybe."

"Let me hear 'em."

I started hitting him with what I'd come up with, ending with the fact that at least one of the cases was being handled by our buddy, Detective Royale.

"And you find that suspicious?"

"You don't?" I asked. "Why didn't he mention it to me?"

"Maybe he figured his name on the report was a dead giveaway."

I stared at Devlin for a few moments, then slumped in my chair.

"Okay," I said, "all the murders took place on the same night. Even in Brooklyn that's unusual, right?"

"I'll grant you that."

"Two victims did not have any fingerprints on file."

"That's not unusual."

"It's not common, Hal," I said. "Most people at one time or another are printed, right? The service, when they're arrested, when they apply for a licence or a job."

"All right, so two out of three victims don't have their prints on file."

I took a breath before hitting him with the big one.

"I think . . . there's a possibility . . . that all three of these murders are connected."

He stared at me. Standing up he said, "You're right, your theory is pretty farfetched."

"I'm not finished, yet," I said.

He sat back down.

"What if Flourish, the man found under the boardwalk, killed Grande?"

"What—"

"Wait," I said, cutting him off. "What if he was then killed by the man they found floating in the marina?"

Devlin shook his head, as if trying to dispel a fog.

"And who killed him?"

"I don't know."

"Well. I'm glad to hear it. I thought you were going to say that Alan Royale did."

I guess I must have looked like I was taking his suggestion seriously, because he stood up and said, "Hey, I'm kidding."

"Yeah, sure," I said. "I know you are, but I'm not."

"On the basis of what you've read in those reports you put this theory together."

"Yep. What I read, and what I surmise, or assume. Remember you said I was allowed to do that in my work?"

"Sure, surmise or assume all you want," Devlin said, "it's a free country, but this is swinging for the fences. Delvecchio, you're trying to hit a grand slam home run and there's nobody on base!"

"Tell me the kind of man who does not have his fingerprints on file anywhere, Hal," I said, trying to bring my last—and probably most farfetched—point across.

"A lot of people don't—"

"But there's one particular type who doesn't. It's what makes him, so special."

He stared at me for a second and then said, "Knowing you, you're talking about a—aw, come on. Delvecchio! Now you're really reaching."

"Right," I said, "a contract killer, a hit man, a mechanic . . . a pro, Hal."

"For Chrissake," Devlin said, "get some sleep, Delvecchio. I'm gonna go and close my eyes for a while."

"Think about it, Hal," I said as he walked out of the room.

"Sleep on it, Delvecchio," he called back, waving at me, "before you say anything to anybody else."

I opened my mouth to answer him, then thought better of it. Sleeping on it didn't sound like a bad idea.

"I still like it," I said to Devlin over breakfast.

He shook his head and then took a bite out of a muffin.

"Delvecchio, you're saying that a pro hit Grande, and then another pro hit the first pro, and then somebody else—maybe a third man—hit the second pro—I'm getting confused talking about it."

"Look. Hal," I said, "you know Jimmy Perlozzo, right?"

"Yeah. I know Jimmy," Devlin said. "He's a snitch."

"Yeah, yeah. I know Jimmy's small time, but he's got one

talent. He knows every hit man on the east coast."

"What if your hit men aren't from the east coast?"

"I'll cross that bridge when I come to it," I said. "If I get Jimmy here and he I.D.'s even one of those victims as a pro, what does that do to my theory?"

"Well . . . that *would* give it some credence."

"I'm going to call Jimmy and get him out here."

"How you gonna do that?"

"By promising him he'll leave here richer than when he came," I said.

"Well," Devlin said, thoughtfully, "that's a lot more than most people get when they come here . . . a helluva lot more."

4

Jimmy had always dressed well for a snitch. When I spotted him at the entrance to the restaurant he was wearing a snazzy blue sports coat, a white shirt with wide, red stripes, a red tie, and light blue pants and shoes to match.

"Jimmy," I said, "as usual you're blinding."

"Good to see you, too, Delvecchio." We shook hands.

"Come on," I said, "let's go get a table."

Jimmy was a bantamweight in his younger days, but had agreed to too many tank jobs. If he had been a little shorter he might have made a good jockey. Now in his late forties he was still in good shape. He might have been taken for a man retired from either one of those sports.

A waiter showed us to a table and we ordered a couple of beers while looking at the menu.

"This is very impressive, Delvecchio," Jimmy said. "Your expense account must be just as impressive."

"It's enough."

"Who's your client?"

"Come on, Jimmy."

"I just thought I'd ask."

We ordered and had another beer each while we waited.

"How long does this hospitality last, Delvecchio?" Jimmy asked.

"One night," I said. "Enjoy it while you can. Check out time tomorrow is as long as you get."

"Should be enough for me to turn whatever you pay me into a small fortune."

"Or lose it."

"Bite your tongue, Delvecchio," Jimmy said. "You forget about the famous Perlozzo luck."

"No," I said, "I was taking that into account."

I waited until after dinner, while we were having coffee, to let him know what I wanted.

"Jimmy," I said, "I need you to identify a couple of stiffs."

He stared at me. "Now? I just ate."

"Look, all I need for you to do is look at a couple of pictures and tell me if you know the guys."

"Morgue photos?" he asked, aghast.

"Better than taking you there, isn't it?"

He thought for a moment and then said, "Let me see the pics."

I took out the morgue photos which had been in with all the reports.

I handed him the photo of Arthur Flourish and he put it on the table.

"Let me see the other one."

I separated the photos of George Grande and the unidentified floater and handed him the photo of the floater. He looked at it, shuddered, then put it down on the table next to the other one.

He stared at them for a few moments, then picked up the coffeepot and poured himself another cup.

"I don't know them."

"Are you sure?"

"Positive," he said. "Do you know for sure that they're pros?"

"No," I said. "I was hoping you'd tell me that."

"Well, either they're not pros, or they're imported talent."

"Damn it."

"Sorry, Delvecchio."

"I know, Jimmy," I said. "It was a long shot, anyway."

I reached for the two pictures and he said, "What's that?" indicating the other I was holding.

"A homicide victim."

"Lemme see."

"I don't really need you to—"

"I'm here I might as well look at everything."

I shrugged, handed him George Grande's photo and the other two.

"Why didn't you show this one to me first?" Jimmy asked.

"I didn't need an I.D. on that one," I said. "The cops know who he was."

"Who was he?"

"Fella named George Grande," I said. "Came here from North Carolina to get himself killed."

"Well I'd swear this was a picture of Ray Guastello," he said.

"Who's Guastello?"

He flicked the photo back at me and said, "He's the hit man you've been looking for, Delvecchio. You wasted your time showing me those first two pictures. Ray's your man."

"Are you sure?"

Jimmy sighed. "Let me look at it again."

I gave him the picture and he stared at it for a few long moments before saying, "That's Ray. What was he doing here?"

"I don't know. It looked like he was gambling."

"That's possible," Jimmy said. "I heard he retired a few years ago."

"Was he any good?"

"As good as some, not as good as others," he said, handing me the photo.

"So what's a retired hit man doing getting killed in Atlantic City."

"Maybe he came out of retirement for a special job."

"Who did he work for?"

"Whoever paid him," Jimmy said, "but he did a lot of work for old man Rienzi."

"Don Vincenzo Rienzi?"

"Yep."

"Jesus," I said. Rienzi and Don Dominick were like oil and water in the old days. Old Don Rienzi was also supposed to be "retired."

"Who's running the Rienzi family now?"

"His son, Anthony."

"From where?"

"Downtown," Jimmy said. "Tony doesn't like the atmosphere uptown."

I put my elbow on the table and my chin in my hand.

"You all right, Delvecchio?"

"Jimmy," I said, "you just opened up a whole new can of worms."

5

Devlin had come up to the suite to take a break from the tables, and I told him what Jimmy had told me.

"The fact that one of these three men was a professional killer does bear out my theory to an extent," I said.

"Delvecchio," Devlin said, "he was killed first. It probably has nothing to do with the other two, and they probably have no connection with each other."

"Hal, what do you know about Tony Rienzi?"

"We in Brooklyn don't have much of an opportunity to mix with the Rienzi's. You have your own connections—"

"I know, Hal," I said, cutting him off. "I know."

"So what are you gonna do?"

"That I don't know."

"What if you just told your client that you couldn't find any connection between his daughter and these murders?"

"Not while I have two days left."

"And if you have nothing at the end of the two days?"

"Then that's what I'll tell him," I said. "That I couldn't find a connection. That wouldn't mean there isn't one, just that I couldn't find it."

"Well, if you tell him there was a Rienzi man here at the same time as his daughter, that might be all he needs to start a war—depending on who he is."

Devlin had not asked me again who my client was but he knew of my association with Dominick Barracondi.

"He's not looking for wars."

"Well, the way these old Dons are, maybe he's not looking for one," Devlin said, "but you may have just found him one."

After Devlin went back to the tables I made a phone call.

"Benny, it's Delvecchio." Benny worked for the Don. We also went to high school together.

"You back from A.C., Nicky?" Benny asked.

"No Benny, I'm calling because I need your help."

"Is this for the Don?"

"Yes, it is."

"Hey, no problem, paisan. What do you need?"

"I need you to tell me whatever you know about the Rienzi family . . ."

"Did you know the Rienzis have a strong foothold in Atlantic City?" I asked Devlin.

He had just come back from the tables, where a run of bad luck had cut into his profits.

"No, I didn't know that. I thought the Conte family had it sewn up. Where did you get the information?"

"From a friend."

"So, what do you intend to do?"

"I'm not sure."

I walked to the window and looked down at the Farley State Marina. The view was so good I could read the names of some of the boats.

"I think I've put it together," I said. "All I've got to do now is make a call and set up a meeting, see what happens . . ."

The person I was meeting chose the Farley State Marina at midnight and wouldn't budge. Since the marina was closed I'd had to climb the cyclone fence to get inside. It was that or swim. I managed to do it without attracting the attention of the single watchman on duty.

I walked among the boats until I found the right one. It was a twenty-foot cabin cruiser, not that I know anything about boats. Written on the bow, in large black letters, was the word "Babe." I had been able to read the name from my window, and it was the last tumbler to click.

"Sorry name for a boat, isn't it?" Alan Royale came into

view on the boat. "I know, I know," he said, "it doesn't show much imagination." His gun was pointing at me.

"Can we get this over with?" I asked.

"What? Don't you want to talk? Like in the movies?"

"I've pretty much figured it out, Alan."

"Well then, let's do a role reversal. Instead of the bad guy telling the good guy the story, you tell me."

"You been on the Conte family's pad for some time, haven't you, Alan?"

"Hell yes," Royale said. "How do you think I can afford this boat? And my clothes?"

"So when you saw Ray Guastello in town you figured you had to do something. You knew he worked for Rienzi, and you knew the Rienzis were trying to move in on the Contes. You wanted to take him out, but you couldn't do it yourself, so you decided to have it done by somebody else—but you didn't want to leave a trail. So, you hired somebody to hire somebody to do it.

"The second killer went into the Showboat and did Guastello, who was registered as George Grande. That man—who had I.D. on him in the name of Arthur Flourish—then went out to the boardwalk to report to the man who hired him. The third man, unidentified to this day, then killed Flourish, leaving him under the boardwalk.

"That leaves us with the third man, who came back here to be paid off by you—and you killed him. Since you were assigned to his murder, you were able to keep him unidentified, and so you thought you were clean."

"And I'm not?"

"There's always a trail, Alan. All I had to do was make some calls to find out you were on Enzo Conte's pad."

"But how did you figure I did the hiring?"

"You were willing to meet me here, weren't you?"

"You mean, if I didn't meet you . . ."

"I guess I would have had to find out another way. Why were you so generous with the reports?"

Royale shrugged and said, "As long as I knew what you were doing I thought I could handle you."

"Tell me, what did Conte think of your plan?"

Royale looked uncomfortable.

"I guess he didn't like it. See, when you're on the pad, Alan, you're not supposed to think, you're just supposed to do as you're told. The cops in New York, they know that real well. You showed some initiative, and what did it get you?"

"I'll tell you what it got me," Royale said. "Embarrassed. Chopped to pieces by that old man in front his Consigliere and his torpedoes instead of the gratitude I deserved— earned."

"So you decided to try and turn a profit from the experience. You decided to blackmail the retired head of one of the New York families? That was ambitious, Alan."

"What the hell . . ." he said with a shrug.

"How did you recognize Carol Dee of the rock group Bad News as Carla Barracondi?"

"I keep a file on wise guys and their families, up here." Royale tapped his temple with his left forefinger.

"Then why didn't your file tell you Guastello was retired? Or that a man like Barracondi wouldn't just submit to blackmail without first looking into the matter?"

"Jesus," he said, shaking his head, "that's what the old man asked me, just before he lit into me."

"That must have been hard to take for a man like you, Alan."

"What do you know? I signed on to uphold the law, and then found out that everybody benefited from what I did but me. I decided to reap some of the profits for myself."

205

"You got greedy this time, didn't you? You've got two family heads, pissed at you. I don't know about Conte, but Barracondi is not going to take it lightly. Especially these old Dons, Al, who still think it's the glory days."

"At least I tried to do something, tried to make something of myself."

"Not that they'd care a whole hell of a lot."

"Sorry, babe, but . . ."

Royale lifted his gun slowly, the way they do in the movies. He'd obviously seen one too many cop or gangster films—or maybe even westerns. When you want to shoot someone you do it quickly, especially from ten feet away. You don't lift your arm, sight down the barrel, take aim and fire. He wasn't on the police range. By the time he brought his arm down, I was in the water. I wanted to shout out in parting, "And don't call me 'babe,' " but my mouth was too full of salt water.

I'm a good swimmer and I was able to make my way to the beach near the boardwalk.

I walked out of the water and sat down in the sand. I looked up at the sky; the moon was full. Luckily, it was a mild night. I decided to just sit for a while. There was no hurry. Once Alan Royale realized I had gotten away, he would probably go on the run himself. When I gave his name to Don Dominick the old man could worry about finding him. Enzo Rienzi would be looking for him, too. Maybe those two old dons would work together.

I'd proven to my satisfaction, and probably to Don Dominick's, that his daughter was not involved with any of the three murders. My job was done. Once I reported my findings I didn't care what happened to the Conte family, the Rienzi family, or Alan Royale.